THE JUNK YARD

THE JUNK YARD

VOICES FROM AN IRISH PRISON

INTRODUCED AND EDITED BY
MARSHA HUNT

MAINSTREAM
PUBLISHING

EDINBURGH AND LONDON

First published in Great Britain in 1999 by
MAINSTREAM PUBLISHING COMPANY (EDINBURGH) LTD
7 Albany Street
Edinburgh EH1 3UG

ISBN 1 84018 217 2

*All royalties will be shared solely amongst the contributors,
who will donate 10 per cent of the overall royalty to the Guild of St Philip Neri,
a prison visitation conference of the St Vincent de Paul Society*

A CIP catalogue record for this book is available from the British Library

Typeset in Garamond
Printed and bound in Finland by WSOY

Shout for all you are worth,
Raise your voice like a trumpet.

Isaiah 58 : 1–9

Acknowledgements

In various ways, scores of people made this project possible, either through what I have learned from them concerning writing, the inspiration that they provide for living, or their direct involvement with my work in the prison.

It seems to be accepted that husbands, wives and partners get thanked last, but in my case, my partner Alan Gilsenan has to be thanked first, because I'm someone who's incapable of leaving my work at the office, so Alan had to listen and advise on the growth of this project every day. In fact, it was his own work in Mountjoy as a documentary film-maker which made it possible for me to ring Vincent Sammon, the head of teaching units for all six Dublin prisons, to ask if I could work with the prisoners. Alan believed that I could teach and from my first day at the prison was full of ideas, advice, encouragement, warning and information which helped me make my Mountjoy experience an adventure. If he found me typing into the night for the prisoners, he might scold me for doing too much, but he also brought me that much-needed cup of tea or coffee. While he was always the first to warn me off providing smokes for the prisoners, he was also the one who bought them duty-free tobacco. When I began collecting new or nearly new books from friends to build up the prison libraries, he endured me turning our entrance hall into a book park. It is due to him that I came to live in Ireland, and it's due to him that I never lost faith in the prisoners or in my growing feeling that their work deserved to be published. He's one of the finest human beings I know and the enormous love he gives has kept me alive and whole.

Vincent Sammon has to be mentioned next, because he gave me the post of writer-in-residence and let me get on with it. In the earliest days of this project, I relied on his knowledge about the prison to form the basis of how I approached my classes and dealt with both the prisoners and the prison staff.

Now I must backtrack and thank many of the editors, agents, publishers and publicists in the book business. In the past fourteen years while I've been writing my own books, I have learned both what to do and what not to do. The prisoners' contributions and the publication of this book benefited from my experience with my own editors over the years. Rosie Cheetham, Alexandra Pringle, Elaine Koster, Andrew Motion, Rebecca Lloyd and John Saddler were important role models for me when I donned my editor's cap. When the time came to find a publisher for the contributors' work, I imitated the likes of agents David Godwin or Abner Stein or Patricia Van Der Leun. In setting up a publicity campaign to launch the book, I pretended I was my good friend Susan Sandon, whose imaginative approach to publicity and marketing served as a blueprint for my own. She works all hours of the day and night, so I did the same. Carmel White has been equally inspiring. Her instinct for publicity is immense and this project has benefited from her involvement in many important ways.

I was imitating my typist Sonia Lane when I'd sit in front of my computer and turn a chaotic page of a story written by someone with a pencil which badly needed sharpening into a print-out from my laptop.

From my first day at the prison, I had to rely on the good will of teachers like Helen Hunt, Anne Costelho, Ciaran Leonard and Tom Lonergan. They advised but more importantly didn't criticise my instincts for sharing my writing experience with the prisoners. I'm grateful to all the teachers for the positive attitude which they created in the school wing. Prison officers in the school wing, especially Officer Declan Lynch, were encouraging with their good will and the respect which they showed the prisoners.

The team at Mainstream Publishing, headed by Bill Campbell and Peter MacKenzie, have been a pleasure to work with and I felt very lucky to have Judy Diamond as my editor. Her calm is persuasive.

I had the extraordinary good fortune to sit next to Rick Stockellburg on a transatlantic flight on 18 March 1999 which changed the shape of the book. He turned out to have editorial skills as well as being a computer buff. Our flight from Gatwick to Boston served as an unbooked editorial session. Many thanks, Rick.

Governor John Lonergan at Mountjoy gave advice and encouragement. That he believes the men and women held in prison have rights and needs that must be addressed sets a fine example not only for the prisoners and staff, but also for others inside and outside the prison. I was most grateful to John for the support which he gave this project. His secretary, Eithne Mulhern, was equally helpful and encouraging when I would appear unannounced, seeking help or information needed for the development and publication of this book.

I thank Jim Murray of the Guild of St Philip Neri, whose agreement to collect and distribute the prisoners' royalties has made it possible to get this book published.

Thanks are also due to Barry Smith of the law firm Richards Butler in London who generously donated his professional time in handling the contributors' book contracts, and to photographer Derek Speirs, Richard and Maggie at Snap Printers in the Sandymount Industrial Estate, Roddy Doyle, Frank McGuinness, Nell McCafferty, Jennifer Johnstone, Christy Dignam, Howard Marks, Maeve Binchy, Gabriel Byrne, John Sutton, Lorcan Ennis, Gerry Smith, Dana Wynter, Kathy Gilfillan, Paul McGuinness, Kitty Murphy, Moira Reilly, Richard and Anne Kearney, Paul Freany, Sheila Byrne, Norman and Declan Heaney, Edward Tobin, Evelyn Conlon, the Village Bookstore at Greystones, Mr Kelly, Mr Lynch, Denise O'Connor, Yellow Asylum Films, Martin Mahon, Gerry Callanan, Pat O'Connor, Stuart Prebble, John Ladner, Iona Skye, my daughter Karis Jagger and her partner Jonathan Watson.

Finally, I thank the men and women of Mountjoy who made my experience so rich and rewarding. When people ask why I don't wish to receive a royalty for my work on this book, I'm quick to explain that I've already been paid in the golden moments that I experienced in the workshops.

I edited this collection making as few changes as possible, and then only in collaboration with the writers.

Go riabh maigh agat.

Introduction

I live in the Wicklow Mountains. From every window I see a spread of nature victorious. Meadows, mountains, forests, fields of sheep or cows grazing, it's a wuthering height of Celtic peace, prosperity and serenity. Snow paints it a breathtaking white. Sun highlights every shade of green, and when this landscape is drenched and blown by violent storms, everywhere speaks of God.

The danger of living here is that in being a writer, I could survive without straying further than the village six miles down the road. Each night I could slip into bed in cosy denial, pretending that this garden of Wicklow, like some postcard, represents all that is Ireland. But, of course, I knew this wasn't true even before I became writer-in-residence at Dublin's Mountjoy Prison. In fact, that's why I wanted the job.

Accepting that life's an account that needs balancing between 'getting this' and 'giving that', I felt I owed something in exchange for the beautiful view outside my windows and other good fortune. I also didn't want to write any more and decided to pass on what I know about expressing myself on the page to prisoners who don't wake to such a rosy dawn. Why prisoners? Because I used to turn my home into a prison of isolation when I worked on a book. Eliminating every temptation that could distract me from writing, I wrote three of my five books alone in an isolated house in France without TV, video, newspapers, magazines or friends, only allowing myself a bit of radio and limited telephone contact. Despite the beautiful views, that house became my cell and writing was my release from the boredom and isolation.

Being an author of fiction and non-fiction, as well as running a successful writing competition for unpublished black writers, I imagined that I'd learned some things about writing which I could share.

Mountjoy is one of the country's main prisons. Brendan Behan, its most famous resident, immortalised it in his 1958 memoir, *Borstal Boy*. It's in a district called Phibsboro, not far from the airport on the busy North Circular Road, and only a ten-minute walk from Dublin's main shopping precinct, O'Connell Street. But someone could pass 'the Joy' every day without knowing that it's there, because it's concealed by the nearly constructed red-brick women's prison. There's no sign of Mountjoy's grim concrete face or the razor-wire trimming its rooftops.

Films and television, books and newspapers have produced images of prison life which I wasn't going to find in the Joy, because although it has the predictable layout of a prison, with cells and cell blocks, only the prison officers wear uniforms and only the men in the training unit eat in a mess hall.

In the main prison, one wing has been designated for education, which is offered as a privilege rather than a prison right. In the separation unit, 'school' is only a single room, and in the women's prison, it's a group of portakabins off the exercise yard. Classes are held from ten to twelve, and two to four, from Monday to Friday, and the term coincides with any normal school term. A class of eight is considered large, and music and art are the most popular. So is cooking, which is taught in a portakabin.

When I began as the writer-in-residence in early October, it was obvious that my three classes (one in the main prison, another in the separation unit, and a third in the women's prison) had attracted people with vastly different abilities. For instance, in the separation unit, two of the ten students had no reading or writing skills at all. So I knew better than to put anyone off with hokum about literature.

'This is not a creative-writing class,' I announced on my first day. 'In fact, I'm not sure what it is. We'll find out as we go along. All you need is paper and a pencil,' I added while handing them out. 'I'm sure I can help you write better letters, and those who want to write more can learn some of the tricks I've taught myself.'

The majority of the men and women were in their early twenties; able, smart, and in the whole of their health. What gradually became clear is that nearly all were (or are) heroin addicts who had stolen to pay for their daily fix. For most, as their stories indicate, their addiction began when they were teenagers.

Loaded with trepidation, I began that first day with a secret weapon: I believe anybody can write if they have something personal to write about. I took it for granted that if I didn't confuse anyone with literary gobbledegook but tried instead to speak their language, I could help some prisoners to discover that writing could be fun and help them endure their sentences. 'Maybe you just want to learn to write a better letter,' I said. But some said that they wanted to write their life story. It wasn't my objective, but I hoped that I'd find at least one person who had real talent.

'Some journalists and scriptwriters make money writing about prisons and the heroin addiction that is your daily life,' I told each group. 'If that's what people want to read about, you lived it, you write it. But only write what you know,' I advised. 'Let the truth tell your story. Start with one memory that stays with you. Something that you feel passionate about.'

The stories which appear in this collection were written over an intense ten-week period. Most deal with an aching, sick, desolate and lonely netherworld of young people trapped between highs. They paint a bleak, fearful mental state that is a junk yard of the mind. The thirty-pound joyride on Heroin the Invincible which rockets them out of it is purpose-built to dump them back again. Yet several admitted that they loved the heroin which buried them alive.

Gradually I saw small miracles; saw men like Demo, who initially joined the class to avoid the yard, take a real interest in writing. I saw Yogi, who said he had hated writing letters, because he had nothing to say, be the first to complete the three-thousand-word target I set for the three groups. (He wrote so honestly about his cold-turkey experience that the men spontaneously applauded when he read it aloud.)

The prison's educational facility is limited. For instance, one twenty-three-year-old's comments showed that he was incredibly wise and observant, but he refused to write a story. What he produced after weeks of cajoling and begging suggested that he was dyslexic. Had he gone through school confused and frustrated about why book-learning and writing came hard? In the local library, a book listed some high achievers like Edison and Einstein with dyslexia. I photocopied it for him, and he brightened when he saw Whoopi Goldberg's name there. When I enquired about getting help for him, I was told that there simply weren't the resources to deal with dyslexia in Mountjoy.

GAINING ENTRY

Outside the blue-painted iron prison doors, I pressed the antiquated bell set into the wall. Everything about the main prison is old, because Mountjoy has been standing in the heart of Dublin since 1850. Being mid-November, it wasn't cold yet, but rain pelted down. It no longer fazes me, because having moved to County Wicklow, south of Dublin, a few years ago, I find rain is as natural to Ireland as sunshine is to California, where my family is based.

I didn't expect the prison door to open quickly. I'd been working three days a week in the prison for several weeks and realised that although more than one prison officer was on the other side for the express purpose of admitting and releasing people, they had to deal with a constant trail, in and out, in and out, in and out, of people coming and going. Solicitors making prison visits. Visitors – from babes-in-arms to elderly parents and grandparents. Prisoners in handcuffs escorted by officers. Teachers, dentists, doctors, social workers, psychiatrists, the clergy, Catholic and Protestant. Officers arriving for duty, others leaving for lunch. Counsellors, gym instructors . . . That blue metal door (personalised by a touch of graffiti) banged day and night. Prison officers studied the faces and credentials of everyone entering and leaving. But activity around ten in the morning, the start of the Joy's school day, tends to be slack.

Standing in the rain, I pressed the bell a second time a little harder, because my watch said 10 a.m. Aware that I was late, I forgot that I was trying to enter a place built to keep some in and others out . . . I rapped on the metal door with my car keys, because I'd seen some guards do it.

When an officer finally admitted me, I stood opposite him in a reception area, a large cubicle of stone walls with iron bars on one side where another officer must open the gate to the forecourt of the prison building itself. The dismal reception is reminiscent of a lion's cage in a Victorian zoo.

The guard's blue eyes studied mine. His uniform was immaculate. Navy sweater and trousers, blue shirt, tie and shiny black brogues. With his close-cropped hair and ruddy cheeks, he could have been a scrubbed Irish rugby player or a Notre Dame quarterback or a redneck, depending on your frame of reference.

I handed him the Ministry of Justice badge with which I had been issued on my first day as a teacher in the prison's education unit. Dark faces like mine are a rarity in Ireland and, with my hair in buns on either side of my head like Princess Leia of *Star Wars*, I look exactly like my ID photo. He scrutinised the plastic-coated badge both front and back and glared at me. 'Who're you?' he demanded. A grunt would have been more civilised. Maybe he was having a hard day.

I've been a lot of things in my life – actress, singer, author, chat-show presenter, mother – and too often I felt that all my credentials needed to be called up whenever I entered the prison, where an unspoken battle of wills exists between the army of prisoners and their guards. Did my being there to help the prisoners imply that I was not on the side of those meant to be on the side of justice? An assistant chief officer once told me, 'We're all part of one family, the prisoners and the staff, and your being here helps us. Because if the prisoners are happy, our job's easier.'

But that morning in the prison reception, late and soaking, I felt for the umpteenth time as if I was being examined like a felon, when 'Who're you?' was jabbed at me. It was hard to remember that every day he does the dirty work that makes it possible for liberals like me to offer the men and women charged with crimes more than a cell under lock and key.

Who am I? 'The writer-in-residence,' I beamed.

'What d'you do?'

I shifted my heavy briefcase from one hand to the other, and, flexing aching fingers, I kept smiling in case he thought he was doing his job. In case everyone without his uniform endures interrogation. But being African American, aggressive, unsympathetic questioning by white officers rankles with me, no matter whose country I'm in. Call it a chip on my shoulder. Call it paranoid. Or call it genetic memory. Whatever it is, with his cold eyes fastened on mine, I was losing patience, and feeling empathy with those who bitch about 'the screws'.

I brushed rain from my forehead. 'I teach the prisoners to write,' I said, 'and I'm already late.'

His aqua eyes were more mocking than his curled upper lip. 'Now I've heard it all.'

I checked my watch. 10.05. I still had to get from reception to the classroom, three more iron gates and three more guards away.

'You a teacher?' he asked.

'A writer.' Having often encountered this sort of interrogation in the prison, I had dressed to look innocuous. But maybe in my fisherman's sweater, jeans and desert boots, I guess I could have been an Angela Davis smuggling in guns. But he didn't check my briefcase.

From a doorway on my right leading to the prison reception came a friendly voice. 'Morning, Marsha.' A grey-haired officer wearing his jacket of rank popped his head out and smiled. It was Mr Murphy, who had stopped me a few weeks earlier to ask me to remind him of the title of a hit record I'd had in 1970. I'm always slightly embarrassed when my past is dredged up, but I also felt relieved that a long-serving officer could call down my old credentials.

'She's okay,' Mr Murphy nodded. I stood between two men who individually represented the best and worst of my exchanges with prison officers. The younger man thrust my badge at me and stepped aside to let me pass. He was just a reminder of something I always told my students: 'I'm an alien in this prison. Not a teacher as such. Obviously not Irish.' It would be several months before I would regularly receive smiles and 'hellos' in return for my own from the prison staff.

In the three-storey wing referred to as 'the school', the atmosphere is relaxed. I felt more at ease amongst friendlier officers stationed in the second-floor corridor. As someone said in my first small class (held on the stage in the auditorium because there was no other place available), 'The Joy is like summer camp compared to most joints.'

The five classrooms have bars on the windows, but otherwise they're no different from those in any grubby institution, and the heavy scent of oil paint drifting from the art studio successfully run by John Robbel makes the school wing practically hospitable.

Raising the window to air my classroom, I noticed the lower roof trimmed with broad spirals of silver razor-wire that glistened in the downpour. Half a dozen bright orange footballs which had escaped from games in the prison yard below were lodged in the wire. They were a harsh reality. I was free to leave, but my students weren't.

KILLING TIME

One Tuesday afternoon, after handing a school officer my scribbled list of the dozen men who had to be released from their cells or the yard to attend my two-hour workshop, I quickly arranged six small Formica tables in a square and set the plastic chairs around it so that the men would sit facing each other. To be ready and appear relaxed when they arrived was important. Unlike others giving classes that afternoon, I was not a teacher, and for everyone's benefit, I insisted that I not be mistaken for one. I expected to use unorthodox teaching methods and didn't want to confuse those taking the accredited English class that the tricks I could share related to writing essays or even a creative-writing class.

On the white board, in black marker, I printed my name, the date and the words 'Killing Time'. That's what we called our workshop. Sometimes there were as many as thirteen men in the group, and I had my work cut out for me, because I'd defied a well-meaning warning from one of the teachers who said, 'Some of the guys might ask you to type their work for them. Don't.'

Call me stupid, but recalling the days when my own typing was so bad that I relied on a typist, I actually offered to type for all twenty-three men and three women spread over my three workshops. It was essential for my own rewrites, so I assumed that it would be essential for theirs. As I told everyone, 'Writing is rewriting. Nobody gets it right first time. First you put down a sketch, then you go back to shade it in with afterthoughts.'

The clarity of a beautifully printed page gave them pride in what they had scribbled in pencil. One hard-face in the separation unit, who admitted that he only joined the workshop to get in out of the cold yard, softened considerably when I returned a page he had scribbled down with his words printed out from my laptop. A couple who had poor spelling and didn't bother to punctuate were so touchingly grateful that it made up for their rowdy behaviour in class. Sometimes stoned eyes, like they were seeing a child being born, stared quietly at the crisp white page full of words in perfect typeface.

'Writing's not about spelling and punctuation,' I had to rant, because a group's energy said that they didn't believe me. 'It's about daring to put yourself on paper. How you feel about something matters. How you describe something is important. But I don't give a shit about how you spell or whether you know how to use commas. Don't let the bogies that got pushed upon you at grade school hold you back. Get your words down the best you can. That'll be good enough.'

I hoped to help some people express themselves better by using the tricks that I'd learned during my fourteen years of struggling without formal training to produce books. 'I made a prison for myself, eliminated temptation so there was nothing to do but write. I moved away from all the disbelievers who thought I didn't have what it takes to write,' I had told them. 'Well, hey, you've got your prison. Now you might as well use it to write.'

My briefcase bulged with the tools I brought to help them do the job: empty notebooks, lined paper, pencils, erasers, loose tobacco and rolling paper, matches, boiled sweets, tissues for runny noses, and a large binder which held the writing a few people had produced before we met. I asked to be shown only what I believed that I could help with. 'Letters. Stories. Diaries. But don't bring poetry, because I'm no poet.'

I brought weird offerings like Edmund White's eight-hundred-page biography of Jean Genet, the French thief who, like Mountjoy's own Brendan Behan, managed to escape his criminal past by succeeding as a writer and playwright. I didn't expect anybody to read Genet's biography, but his pug-nosed image on the hardback cover helped them remember that criminals can be writers too.

That Tuesday afternoon, as I placed the tobacco, skins, matches and sweets in the centre of the square, my favourite prison officer, Mr Lynch, who treated the prisoners decently, stuck his head in the door. 'Bribing 'em again, eh?' he jibed. Although I didn't see the tobacco and sweets as bribery, I'm sure a few people assumed my workshops had a high attendance for just that reason. But since I rely on mints when writing gets tough, I wanted the prisoners to have my advantage. And, as for the tobacco, I couldn't help but notice during the first workshop that a few derived pleasure from rolling a fag. I wondered if others were having a nicotine fit while the guy beside him smoked.

There's tons about writing that I don't know, but one thing's definite: writers who smoke, smoke while they write. So I started bringing the necessaries for roll-ups, to make sure that everyone who wanted to smoke could do so without asking. I even suggested that people not bother bringing their own. I forgot that I'd have to keep this up, and not only was it expensive with six, and sometimes seven, sessions per week, but I had to remember to stock up. Eventually, of course, some of the men got so spoiled that I got complaints about the Glacier mints . . .

Before this starts sounding like one long party, let me say that in the beginning I felt like one of those teachers in a school run by gangs. I never felt personally threatened, but in the early days, I would stand at the board in front of inmates slumped in their chairs, doodling or whispering to the person beside them and eyeing me with blatant derision. As a performer, I had learned to judge my audience, so I had no delusions. In the women's prison in particular, my first session felt like a tough audition. Twelve women sat in a portakabin fitted out like a kitchen. Cooker, sink, fridge, the lot, with me trying to explain with enthusiasm why taking my writing workshop was worth them leaving their cells.

Trust had to be built a roll-up at a time. I gave all three groups exercises that seemed ridiculous, even to me, but I was always operating on instincts, asking them to do the do-able. 'Write about what you had for breakfast,' I told the men in the main prison. They gaped at me like I was nuts. 'G'won. Write.'

One kid raised his hand. 'I had nothin'. Coffee and a roll-up.'

'Okay. So write that,' I said.

He looked at me, peered at the kid across from him, shook his head in dismay and started writing. Next I asked the group to write about that same breakfast to a relative or friend, somebody they really liked, that they could talk straight to. One man, John Maloney, who was released from prison after my first session wrote:

'Dear Father,
I had a nice bowl of cornflakes

and a delicious cup of coffee,
Love, John.'

I picked up his notebook and glanced at the neat printing. 'You decided to write to your dad?' I was impressed.

'No, it's the priest.' The class laughed. I joined them. Often they were entertained by my naïveté, my Americanness, my blackness, my ghetto straight-talk or various combinations of the four.

'Okay . . . and what about this delicious cup of coffee? Was it really delicious?'

'Fuck, no, it tasted like shite.' The class of thirteen roared, and my response probably surprised them.

'Well, can you please write that,' I said. 'And if the priest isn't somebody that you can be totally straight with, find somebody else to write to, because rule number one, two and three is that if you write honestly, it'll always be more interesting. How would you tell it to a friend . . . that's your audience.'

The smokes and sweets were evidence that I genuinely wanted people to feel relaxed and enjoy the sessions. For some, to roll a fag, unwrap a boiled mint and enjoy both with the lads helped to establish the workshops as a gathering where they were expected to speak their minds. 'There're a couple rules: you're not allowed to laugh at anything anybody writes or says. You'll know when something's meant to be funny, then you can laugh.'

They liked me to talk tough.

For a kid of twenty who'd slopped out his cell at nine and endured some humiliation by ten, looking forward to killing time with a mint, a roll-up and the lads in our workshop may have been his lifeline. I wanted to forget that some of them had committed serious crimes. But I needed to remain impartial, and therefore refused to know why anyone was serving time, because I didn't want to feel fear or be prejudiced.

Prison is their penalty. With each tick of the clock, they pay.

FUCK THE BEGRUDGERS

A November sun was shining. The sky was cloudless blue. I was setting up for my Tuesday tutorials. As important as it was to develop work in a group, when I had more than one person's writing to consider, it was impossible to give individual help to someone who needed to discuss a developing story. So on Tuesday mornings in the main prison where I had my largest workshop, I held one-to-one tutorials.

Ali Baba was due in at ten, but Fiddler had popped by first. 'Fidget' could be his other nickname, and I had a lot of time for him, because he was the first, along with Penner and Puma, whose early enthusiasm and respect helped to establish me as credible. During the early workshops, Fiddler and Puma looked after me, making sure that nobody nicked the tobacco and that I left the classroom with whatever I'd come with.

I was writing on the board with my back to the room when the blank paper which I'd placed on the table started to blow about in the breeze. Without turning around, I shouted, 'Hey, Fiddler! Close that bloody window, the papers are blowing about.' He invariably complained about the heat and usually rushed into the workshops and immediately started raising the windows. 'You're not even supposed to be here. Where's Ali Baba?'

'I think he's got cookin'. It's fucking boilin' in here.'

Fiddler was grinning beside the window, which he'd propped open with an old roller-blind. As usual he was wearing cotton shorts although, despite the bit of autumn sunshine, it was hardly the temperature for them. I valued him as one of the most eager and talented of the prisoners. The piece he wrote about his confirmation had been an ice-breaker in the workshop. The afternoon he'd read it, the class laughed at the right moments and erupted in spontaneous applause when he'd finished. It gave the others confidence, because they assumed that if he could write, so could they.

Fiddler was a Curtis Mayfield fan and was always trying to hit me up for a Curtis Mayfield tape, dropping hints or making a request outright. Much as I wanted to give in to him, I resisted, because both he and the others would have dismissed me as a sucker. In subtle ways, they were always testing me, and maintaining their respect was tantamount to whether I'd get them to take my writing tips seriously.

'Fiddler, we absolutely cannot have papers blowing about the room,' I repeated. 'And how many mints did you take?' There were a good deal fewer than I'd set out.

'Whatch'ya writin'?' he blurted in that Dublin accent which often meant that I couldn't understand what he or the others said.

'"Fuck the Begrudgers".'

The word 'fuck' wasn't exactly pejorative. It spoke paragraphs one minute and was a comma between phrases the next. In the workshops, it was the most far-reaching, liberating, albeit overused word shared between us. It became password, salute, plea and defecation. 'Fuck' at various junctures said 'I love you', 'I hate you' or 'I trust you'. 'Fuck' could signal a new friendship or rupture an old one. The problem is that in writing, it's a bit like salt is with food. Too much can kill good dialogue and murder a good story.

Any outsider who came into the workshops might have been appalled because the men wore the word down. I was certain that it contributed to an atmosphere of honesty and exorcised the ghosts of grammar, punctuation and spelling which can hang over a classroom.

'Fuck the begrudgers' became our motto, our battle-cry. I'd say, 'The begrudgers are everybody and everything that sits on your shoulder telling you that you can't write. Be it conscience, an old schoolteacher, a relative, a lover, or the officers outside in the corridor. So fuck 'em and keep writing. What you have to say is important and hasn't been said before. When we write honestly, we usually say what many may think but wouldn't dare commit to paper.'

That November morning, I wanted to ask Fiddler who his begrudgers were, because I knew he was suddenly finding it impossible to write. He put it down to a new cell-mate, and how could I challenge that when I personally can't write if there's someone in the room? Most people need isolation to apply themselves to thinking the thoughts that come from the deep.

Fiddler also put his block down to our workshops, and I was ready to believe that too much talk about writing can stop someone from doing it.

'You think I've given you too much to think about?' I asked. 'Is it the classes that are fucking you up?'

Fiddler looked at me. 'Yeah. Maybe. The most helpful thing you told me was to find somebody to write to. The rest is getting me confused. I'm thinking too much.'

'Writing to a friend helps the way you tell something to remain consistent. In literature, they call it "finding a voice". But you know what I think has happened with that story about your last prescription? One minute you're writing to a friend, and the next, it feels like you're writing to me.'

'I *am* writing to you.'

'That's no good. You don't know me well enough and you keep throwing in words that seem like they're meant to impress. Just say what you have to say to some friend who'd be able to read the page and say, "That sounds just like you." And get rid of the begrudgers who say that you can't write, or that you're not smart enough to write or that you haven't got a worthwhile thing to say. "Fuck the Begrudgers" and see if you can find Ali Baba for me.'

He headed for the door after grabbing another mint. 'I could really use some new sounds. Bit of Curtis Mayfield.' The others sometimes called him 'the hippy'.

PENNER'S FORTIETH

Maybe he wanted to forget that he was turning forty. But suppose he didn't? Penner was our senior citizen. Almost everyone else was in their twenties.

I stood in a Phibsboro bakery two blocks from the prison, trying to decide whether I was doing the right thing getting Penner a cake. He was my most hard-working student. A writing natural. Maybe he should have been writing for a popular newspaper. The stories just rolled out of him.

Only a few days before his birthday, I pleaded, 'How am I gonna make you understand that writing is rewriting, Penner? It's great that you've produced seventeen more pages, but you *have* to stop and make sure that you don't need to remove something or add something else.' I was desperately worried that I was misguiding him. I'd take my morning walk and be thinking, 'Suppose Penner has a future with Mills and Boon and you're crushing a natural talent?'

I had to renegue on my promise to type what was submitted by the students, because Penner handed in so many. I felt badly about it, but as it was I was up all hours and even typed at weekends and during lunchbreaks to stay on top of people's writing and rewriting.

At the bakery counter I studied the cakes. It was a toss-up between the chocolate layer and the Black Forest gateau with fresh cream. I couldn't decide whether the group would prefer the delicacy of the fresh cream cake or the sugary weight of the layered chocolate, the sort they'd probably enjoyed growing up. It was impossible to forget that most were hardly more than children.

At the sweet shop I picked up birthday-cake candles, skins, matches and gift wrap. I already had the gift: F. Scott Fitzgerald's *The Great Gatsby*. Like Gatsby, Penner, as one of his stories told, was driven by his love for a woman.

Happy Birthday to you,
Happy Birthday to you,
Happy Birthday dear Penner . . .

Everybody sang and he blew out the ten candles. I removed them from the cake and placed them on the table while I cut it. When I went to put them in my bag, I noticed a few were missing.

'Who nicked the candles?' I asked as the eight men scoffed great wedges of chocolate cake. There's was a lot of laughter and blushing. 'Come on, you bastards. I'm not that green. I know what you're up to.' The personal memories that most of them had been working on dealt with scoring heroin ('gear', as they called it) or getting high, because when asked to produce true stories that they felt passionately enough to write three thousand words about, the heroine was usually heroin . . . So I was well schooled in how gear gets heated and I suspected that the little birthday candles might go for cooking up some heroin on a landing.

When everyone had eaten, I suggested that we do one of the early exercises I used to give them. 'Everybody write a line or two about that remaining piece of Penner's birthday cake, and then let's see what the group comes up with jointly. Write only what is honest. Don't try to be tricky or clever. Just be honest, and remember, the simplest statement is often the best.'

With hindsight, I can see that early on the value of this exercise was that everyone got used to writing about something on demand and reading it aloud. I asked them to write simple, clear statements about an inanimate object which they all had some relationship to, like an empty sweets packet in the centre of the table. Then, one by one, everybody would read their few lines aloud. It was exciting to hear what everyone else had to say, and any who had been painfully shy during the early workshops were less timid by the later weeks. In fact, by the time of Penner's fortieth, it was obvious that this exercise was no longer demanding enough for the group. A few of them, though, like Ali Baba, made little statements that seemed touchingly true and well thought-out.

Here's what they came up with which Terry jotted down in Penner's birthday card:

> There's a scrumptious piece of birthday cake on the table. The candles are gone. It sits alone on a silver tray. Penner is exactly forty years older than that cake. It's brown with cream, sponge, and more cream. Marsha wanted one slice for the screw. The base of it reminds me of my Ma's wedding photo.

THE WRITING ON THE WALL

A very nice Irish editor who turned down publishing this collection said, 'Too many of the stories have a similar theme.'

'That's their collective importance,' I retorted. 'All these young people have written similar stories because the memory they can most passionately relate is a drug experience. Yet they get too little social support to get free of their predicament. You wouldn't tell somebody possessed by a demon, "Pull your socks up, will you, and get rid of him!"'

Over our ten weeks of sessions, several of my students were obviously on heroin when they came to the workshop. How am I sure? They were scratching and nodding, or slurring with that absent look in their eyes that I'd seen often enough when I was in the rock'n'roll business. I wanted to ask, 'How exactly do drugs get into the prison at such a rate that you can stay high?' Instead I once said at the beginning of an afternoon workshop, 'Don't think I haven't noticed that some of you come to class out of your minds on smack, and I just hope you're using clean needles.'

The response?

One person chuckled, 'Clean needles, me fuckin' arse. Sometimes there's only one for a whole block.'

'And how many to a block?'

'Eighty.'

'You're bullshitting me, right?'

They liked to get a rise out of me, but on this occasion, I was so afraid they were telling the truth, I was silent.

In my briefcase was a tabloid article which Ali Baba gave me to read about death row in Texas. I was tempted to pass it around the class and say, 'Using the same needle turns this place into a death row.' But I didn't because I was constantly aware that these people had to return to their cells where they might sit alone and think themselves into a stink . . . For all I knew a few of them might have shared a needle that very afternoon.

Chambers Dictionary says a junk yard is 'a place where junk is stored or collected'. Why has prison become a dumping ground for drug addicts? They are part of our society, and who among us can forget that we're all in the insidious heroin chain? Take the Dublin 4 housewife, who can't leave home without switching on the burglar alarm, or the grandfather in Ballyfermot who was mugged by two teenagers desperate to buy the next ride out of the junk yard. And what about that art student working part time in a Dun Laoghaire record store – should he forget that day he had a dirty syringe held at his throat until he handed over the money in the till? And how about the Cork family who buried not one but two of their children, dead from shooting up? Will they ever forget?

What I taught is minor. The voices it freed are major. They sing a strangled and haunting tune with a repetitive refrain. Like Gotzy says, 'Drugs drugs and more drugs.' So instead of complaining that the themes are the same, ask why so many have a similar tale to tell. Not about the Celtic Tiger or the Celtic Spirit, but about how gear can possess a body and soul.

I am very proud to present this collection. The stories are true, although names may be changed to protect the writer or others. The seventeen contributors had to dredge up truths that must have been hard to face alone in their cells. I salute their bravery.

Marsha Hunt
Co. Wicklow
April 1999

Contents

CHILDHOOD

DEMO

"THE WORLD COULD BE A BETTER PLACE"
YESTERDAY is HISTORY TOMORROW is A mystery
AND Today I'm STill ALive".

To my grandparents - who I've always called Marda - all my love for a great childhood - and many thanks to Marsha for inspiration!

My life began on 23 June 1969 which was the day I was born and the same day I was baptised due to some sort of trouble and on account of a priest being there to give me my last rites, because I was dying.

I know all of this as I was told by my mother who is the best mother anyone could have!

Although all I recall, one day I was maybe three or four years old, my mum took me to the shops and bought me a pair of boot runners. I was delighted with me runners, 'cause I was the only one with them. None of my friends had them. I remember it; I was the hero with all my friends for that day.

And then that evening as my Ma was going out as I thought like any normal kid would, I saw her at the end of our street, so I was calling her, 'Ma! Ma! Mammy . . .' And just then as I was running towards her and getting closer, I could see she had a pound note in her hand which she gave me to spend in the shop for me and my friends. And as she bent down to do one of my laces, I noticed little tears in her eyes.

'What's wrong, Ma?' I asked in my little boy voice.

'Nothing, son. It's just the wind, son.'

'Okay, Ma.'

'Okay, son . . . David? . . .'

'Yes, Ma?'

'Go the shop with your friends and buy some sweets and share them.'

'I will, Ma.'

And she gave me a kiss and a hug and told me to mind crossing the road.

I told me Ma, 'I will, Ma . . . Okay, Ma, Ma . . . Mam?'

'Yes, son?'

'Bye, Ma.'

'Bye, son.'

And she had those tears again as she went away.

I never saw her until years later. I was about nine years old.

FIDDLER

This book is a miracle and so are the eels that
wrote it - Masha Hunt the most compassonete unassuming
Deneford human being made it all possible - we love her.
I loved to say some profound but all I can say is
we pulled it off Nice Fuck the sheep and beware of followers

Dene Farrell : to daddy whom I never knew - to mommy
who is the very Air I breath and to all people who
Are being done injustice to, do not be a victim, you have
Power.

It's a scorcher of a summer's evening.

I can't remember the details but I know you're gone.

Gone to work.

But it feels to me as if you're never coming back. It always feels like that. As if part of my inside has been cut away and only you can replace it. I only recall and wonder now if Robbie and Denise ever felt this separation.

I remember . . . I am in the terrace with Anto Jackson. All the other kids are out playing. I'd say they are happy with their Ma and Da at home. You're at work. A million miles from me. The pain . . . The feeling I can't escape. I have to be with you and can hear a song in my head; one that I think I heard earlier on the radio. 'Johnny comes home from the fair . . .' Or something . . . I just want to burst into tears on the ground, helpless. But I know that still won't make you be there. So I run. I tear over the terrace wall running to you. (You brought me to work before, and although I have not worked out where streets are, I know where you will be like a built-in radar. You work cleaning that spark plug office in Grafton Street . . . the smell of pipe tobacco and the clock with the spark plug in it . . . all the empty offices. And I would sit on the Man's chair pretending I was just like him. The feeling you get when you're in someone else's space is weird. But you were just cleaning. Wanting to get the job done.)

I never seen you working in my strange quiet world.

I remember the smock you have on, a purple yoke with flowers on it.

You're only thirty-five and left a widow with me and my brother and sister.

To me you are God.

You bring me around to Dawson Street. Another cleaning job. It's a bank but feels more personal. Your two friends work here. Kaye and Miss – I forget her second name – was it Preston? I think she's dead now, but she was so nice. And Kaye is still your friend. (She is lovely. She's so understanding. Youse were meant to meet, to be great friends.) Two people live upstairs over the bank. They're friends as well. The man fixes everything in the bank and I think that's why they stay there.

I always see the big lift when I walk in and the stairs beside it. I think we always used to take the stairs, but I remember when I used to play when you are cleaning, I got stuck in the lift one night and youse were all telling me to press buttons and everything. I felt so helpless. Then the man came. Tony or something. And as soon as I heard his voice, I felt I was safe. I was so lost, I scraped all the skin off my scalp till it bled.

I can smell them lifts and buildings.

On Friday we get paid.

Kaye always chews PK Chewing Gum. The little ones that you get four in a pack. 'Member you used to buy me a pack to give her? It felt great giving her to them. (She is so like you.)

We go to Dunnes Friday. Late shopping. It has big, huge windows at the side and I can see everything. All the shelves. The cash registers. And the people putting stuff in plastic bags.

CHOCO

Dedicated to my mom, dad and daughter Jade, who inspired, supported and help me through my darkest hours of jail time...

Choco xxx.

'It's not fuckin' fair! Why do I have to go to bed early and everyone else stays up!' Tracey's head turned as I raised my voice. She was six years old.

A worried kind of look came onto my Ma's face. 'Please John, ya know what your father's like. Just go up for me. I can't take the pressure.' She was sitting in the sofa-chair across from the telly. Chain-smoking Silk Cuts. The curtains were pulled to keep the heat in the room. Tony was sitting on the couch glued to Bruce Forsyth and the bit-o'-stuff with the big tits beside him. 'Brucie's Bonus' was always on of a Thursday. There wasn't much else for my younger brother or sister to watch on these cold winter nights.

I could feel the blood rising to my face as I tried to think of why I was being asked to go up to the fuckin' bedroom at nine-thirty while both me younger brother and sister were able to stay up watching television. But I didn't really need to ask why. I already bleedin' knew.

Boom!! The sitting room door slammed behind me, and I'm sure the neighbours three doors down could hear me stomping my way upstairs. My hands were opening and closing in frustration.

I was fifteen years old and my father was due home some time in the next three hours, drunk and aggressive. It had been this way for as long as I could remember. It would happen at stages and at different times. Like at the dinner table, somebody would ask where the old fella was . . . 'Ma, where's Da?'

'He's gone to the bookie's. But ya know your father. He's probably met some shower of shite he calls friends and gone to the pub. Don't turn off the cooker tray, in case he's back soon. He'll only be giving out about a cold dinner.'

'Fuck him. Fuckin' scumbag!!'

'That's enough, John. Why give him an excuse?'

'Why give him an excuse'. Jaysus, if I had a penny for every time I heard that growing up, I'd be like that fuckin' pond in the ILAC Centre . . .

It didn't really matter anyway. He would always find an excuse. Sure, weren't his two biggest excuses sitting right here this very moment arguing over keepin' his bleedin' dinner hot? Me or Ma. Ma or me. Always one or the other.

I'd only become a target in the last couple of years. He had turned his drunken attack and abuse towards me, as he faced a couple of years behind bars if he attacked me Ma. So along with every electrical appliance in the house, I became a legitimate target, and as I stomped my way across the landing to my bedroom, I made my decision. 'Get the fuck out of here quick.'

'Ya can't go to London.'
  'Who fuckin' can't?'
'Ya can't go. You're too young.'
Me and Tony's bedroom was a small boxroom with bunks. I always had choice of which bed to sleep in being older and all that. Though Tony let me push 'im around a bit, he'd not let it go too far. Like if I gave him a good clatter, he'd get stuck in flying at me with kicks and punches. He was a big twelve-year-old who was in the boxing club, so a good hook off 'im hurt.
  'Lookit. I'll be sixteen in a few weeks and I can do what I like.'
  'No, ya can't. Ya can't buy gargle.'
  'Are you gettin' cheeky?'
  'But ya can't. And ya can't go see *Basic Instinct*.'
  'Who can't! Didn't I get in to see *Freddy*? And don't I get served in Apple Annie's? And what the fuck has gettin' into the pictures got to do with me going to fuckin' London anyway, Tony. There's nobody standing in bleedin' Holyhead with a ticket clipper asking you for student ID, ya wanker!!'
  'Ah, fuck off. You know everything, don't ya!'
  'Listen, ya little prick, I know one fuckin' thing, and that's you're a little lick arse bastard who'll be outta fuckin' bed and down the stairs as soon as ya smell the chips that fuckface brings home. I won't get any, will I? The only sniff of fuckin' chips I'll get is when he gets pissed off abusing Ma and comes upstairs to bully fuckin' me. Now shut your little arse lick mouth or I'll really go to town on your head. I'm going to London and nobody is going to stop me. Not you. Not Ma. Not the fuckin' police. NOT THE LEGION OF FUCKIN' MARY, THE U.S. MARINES, NOBODY! Do ya hear me!!!'
  'Okay, okay. Stop shouting! You'll wake Tracey.'
  'John Brennan, what are you shouting for!' My mother's voice would not be loud but strong enough just to be heard in our room. 'It's bad enough having your father to deal with without you starting!'
  'Look,' said my brother, 'your nose is bleeding.' This was

another thing that had happened as far back as I can remember. Any time I got really annoyed, my nose would start dripping blood like a leaky tap. 'Here, wipe your nose. It's all over your pyjamas.'

It was getting late and I knew the old fella would be home shortly. I got down off the top bunk and headed towards the toilet for some jacks roll to plug me leaky nose with, and coming back I turned the small table lamp off and bounced into the top bunk again.

'Goodnight,' Tony chimed off.

'Goodnight.'

'Goodnight,' Tony said again, catching on that I was trying to get the last word in.

'Goodnight,' I replied, kicking myself for starting this head game in the first place. It could go on like this for about three quarters of an hour with both of us trying to be the one to get the last word. Tony always won, and looking back, it was his head-strong attitude towards my father that kept him out of trouble with Da. Tony could hate him without showing it, whereas my contempt for him would be sprayed all over my face.

I awoke in the morning feeling fit and rested. As always on mornings like this, the first thing I'd think was, 'Well, the old man must have been too drunk to start any trouble last night.' I blasted the stereo in me room as I began to dress.

'John, Stuy's at the door!' I thought I heard somebody shout. But with the music blasting away, I couldn't be sure. Then, 'JOHN! Stuy is at the fucking door and lower that bleedin' radio.'

'I'll be down, now!'

Stuy was and is my best friend. For as long as I can remember, we've been confidants. For years we'd gone to the same schools, got into the same trouble, and eventually we both got fucked up on gear together. We were chalk and cheese to look at, me being dark with black hair and a thin build, and Stuy being blond and stocky.

I bounced down the stairs. It wasn't normal for Stuy to be up before twelve when he wasn't working.

'All right, Stuy, what's happening?' I said opening the door.

'Ah, fuck all. Ya comin' down the shops?'

'Hang on, and I'll see if me Ma wants anything in the shop.'

'No love.'

It was one of those winter days where the sky is clear, and it looks bright and warm but is really fucking freezing. I grabbed my coat and slammed the front door after me.

'So, did you meet her last night, Stuy?' I asked as he offered a smoke.

'Yeah.'

'And . . . ?'

'And what?'

I grappled with a gammy lighter trying to light me smoke and keep up with Stuy's fast pace. 'Hold on,' I asked, and we both stopped. He offered me the burning end of his and I lit mine off it. 'So did you ride her?'

'Leave it out, will ya.'

'Ha, Stuy, I bet ya didn't even drop the hand.'

'That's for me to know and you to find out.'

'Go on outta that. I'm only winding you up. She's a nice bird and I wouldn't mind giving her one.'

'You'd want to leave it out!'

I changed the subject. 'I'm really thinking of going to London, Stuy.'

'Are ya?'

'Yeah.'

'When?'

'As soon as possible.'

'Why?'

'Ah, you know yourself, the oul' fella and all. It's wreckin' me head. He's saying now that I have to be in at half nine. And when he's on the piss, me Ma sends Tony out lookin' for me, so I'm there when Da comes in, 'cause he locks the door whether it's nine-thirty or not.'

'Yeah, he's a right cunt when he's drink on him. But goin' to London's a bit much, isn't it?'

'Not really, Stu, 'cause Sam and Dave are over there and I can bring a few birth certs over and get a couple doles going. Fuck it, it'd be better than staying here going through this crap.'

'Ah, it'll blow over soon enough.'

'Nah, Stu. This is it. Do or die! I can't take any more, so I'm fuckin' off full stop.'

Although Stuy would waffle along with me about this idea of going to London, he also knows what a cunt I am for exaggerating things. And I know at this point in my planning for this trip, Stuy put the whole idea down to pure fantasy on my part. After all, I was fifteen and fifteen-year-olds talk hard, act hard but generally do what most other fifteen-year-olds do; go to school, smoke hash, and try and ride any bird that will let them.

They don't on the spur of the moment fuck off to one of the biggest cities in the world.

But I did.

FIDDLER

I Love to say something profound but buy this
book and your life will be better and mine richer but
seriously if you want it from the mouth this is the book to
read not just another middle class attempt at writing about crime
+ drugs a real thing, also stops more humans to.

I Decidicate this bode to my Father whom I never know
my mother who is my lifes Breath and last but not
least to all the kids who took part

My experience of making my confirmation, whatever that means, was a fucked-up day from the start. I was physically sick and shitting every five minutes. My eyes were puffed up and I felt drained. I came downstairs in a daze knowing that this was my day. My twenty-four hours. Today I was the Centre of Attention in my house. But I would've rather gone back to bed. What a day to get sick. I'd slept in the back bedroom with me big brother. Me Ma and aunty were waiting in the front room for me to blow dry me hair and clean me up. But I wasn't into it. I didn't like the attention. I was uncomfortable with it. I was a shy twelve-year-old.

The lights were on even though it was nine in the morning. There was a chair in the middle of the room for me to sit on.

Me aunty was me godmother. She was always smiling and she's the image of me Ma. I think the two of them were separated at birth. She was always around for anything that was happening for me. She was the only one who had a hair dryer, so she could style hair, or at least she thought she could.

My haircut was well retro. One of those hairdos you see on the seventies posters in the barber's. They'd use footballers for models. Like you'd see Kevin Keegan with a bleedin' bowl-shaped, fuzzy Afro.

Me aunty thought she was doin' a Barbie Doll up. Rollin' the hair around the brush. I was sittin' there in me jocks, and the suit was hangin' on the wall on a hanger. Me aunty gave me it and says, 'Put that on.'

The suit was like wallpaper with a bullet stopper tie and a silk hanky for the pocket. Nobody knew how to put a knot in the tie and your woman next door had to come in and do it. Ellie next door, she was ancient. Used to always wear one of them house-cleaning bibs. I think she knew how to tie knots, because her brother always wore a tie to the pub. He was ancient as well.

I had a pair of tan George Webb's which were two sizes too big. You see, they only came in size six, and I only took a four. But a couple of *Evening Heralds* would take care of that . . . I had two pair of stockings on as well. Me legs were like plaster of Paris.

So off to the church I go like a large piece of my Granny's wallpaper with shoes. On the way round to the church, there were people everywhere. It was sunny out and I was starting to feel a bit better.

The church was just around the corner from me house, but I

had to go to the school first. We met a tribe of people at the Donnellys' house. Richard was making his confirmation as well. Me and him got together and shot around to it, so me Ma waited in the church for me with me aunty, of course.

We all had to meet in the yard, because everybody who was making their confirmation had to go to the church together. When we got there, you could feel the excitement. They used to keep watch dogs in the yard. Big Alsatians. One was called Shane, and they used to piss and shite all over it. I'll never forget that smell. We were waiting on the brother, the Christian brother. I forget his name.

Everyone was checking out each other's clobber, and especially Ger Shanahan's. A salmon-pink suit. He was always a bit trendy, but this time he went well off. I think as well that it was the first time one of our age had worn some type of perfume, because he smelt like me Ma's lipstick bag.

The twenty blokes were all standing around dressed up in mad suits. All smoking. Thinking we were great. Then we went to the church.

I used to love the smell of frankincense and a few paintings, but other than that, churches were dead.

I have a vague memory of the ceremony; I never took the pledge to abstain from alcohol, because I was going gargling that night. (I think the pledge was introduced 'specially for the Irish.)

We were called up to take our confirmation names. I took Ian. I suppose the bleedin' bishop thought it was after St Iain, but it was after Ian Dury, the patron saint of drugs and rock'n'roll, which was a road I would later dedicate my life to.

So up we go to the bishop to get the names. He was like a character out of *Spitting Image*, sitting there half asleep in all his glorious senility. He was giving out some blessing, saying some prayer. I felt like saying, 'I'm only in this for the money.' I couldn't wait for it to be over.

After the church, we're all out in the grounds having photos taken. And to this day, I still have one of myself, Richie Donnelly and Noel Murray. Noel is dead now from the virus.

Geez, I hope I still have that photo.

We all had the same mad hairdos and wallpaper suits, and the three of us are standing there. The look on our faces in the photo is hard to describe. False smiles. We look so young. Time goes so fast. People are gone . . .

The tradition of making confirmation is after the church business, your Ma brings you around to visit your relatives where you get the money. Wanga Spondollocks!

You visit cousins you've never seen in your life and pretend to be shy and bashful, hoping they give you a decent few bob. If you hear the clinking of coins, your heart hits the ground.

It was heavy work trudging around Dublin all day: Finglas, Ballymun, Inchicore. Me brother and me sister came with us as well. Just tagging along. But I was lucky there were eighteen in my Ma's family. Plenty of rich pickings.

It was great getting home to get that mad suit off me. They're a waste of money, because you only wear them once. It's not as if we were bursting with money, because my mother was left a widow at twenty-four with three of us and had to work just to keep us in basics.

I remember going to town to buy the suit. She must have saved for ages. My Ma was great at that. She always got the money. I don't know how, but she was a fucking miracle maker. She would always treat us like royalty.

DEMO

i'm smiling it's WENSDAY MORNING
AND MARSHA is coming in to class
today i look FORWARD to wensday
MORNING it's Like getting a visit
cause i feel light after the
class it breaks my week up

I started to take drugs at the age of fourteen. My friends were all strung out months before me. I was taking assorted tablets like DF-118s and valium and hash. At first it wasn't every night. After at least a month, it became an everyday thing.

I started to depend on valium. I used to wake up and swallow at least ten or twelve tablets with a cup of tea and a smoke. Then I'd leave my gaff and I'd sit on the stairs and make a joint and then the valium would take effect. When stoned on valium, you'd be feeling bullet-proof. Ya don't feel any pain. Like if ya got a bang off a pole, ya wouldn't feel it, and ya feel like a bullet would bounce off ya. I swear they just took over me. I used to get very violent on them as well.

All this lasted for a year or two.

And three days after my sixteenth birthday, I was arrested and taken off a bus by the police, because I had warrants for not appearing in court on charges for burglary. The garda waited until I was gone past my sixteenth birthday, 'cause they couldn't hold me anywhere except St Patrick's Institution.

I was sentenced to twelve months in St Patrick's.

I was a bit upset when I was first locked up, but after a few days, I was getting used to it. But my Ma was very upset. She thought I was in a cell with murderers and rapists, so I had to reassure her that everything was okay and I was doing fine.

I got through my twelve months, no problem. But then the nightmare started when I got out.

I used to stay in a flat with a few old friends. We went through our teenage years together, spent years taking drugs together and we are still friends today.

Now that flat was a right shooting gallery. We used to drink cider and smoke hash and take all kinds of drugs. And we sold hash and robbed people's houses.

All my friends (I got a shock when I saw this), they were injecting drugs. I nearly got sick, 'cause I never even seen anybody banging up in a movie. This was 1986 and the AIDS virus was only breaking news.

I was offered it a few times and I said no at the time. I was still taking valium, DF-118s, hash, and I was snorting morphine tablets.

As time went by, I kept it up. Stoned all the time, day in and day out.

One day I couldn't get any of the fucking drugs I was abusing.

I was standing in the shopping centre for hours trying to buy drugs. But the only thing on offer was heroin. I didn't realise at the time, because I didn't know what withdrawal symptoms were, but I was going through the motions of the withdrawals. I felt tired and my senses were lacking. I wasn't fully alert and my body just didn't feel like mine.

One of my friends came up to me and said, 'What's the story? Are ye sick?'

'No.'

He said, 'You look sick.'

Heroin was forty pounds a bag at the time and he asked me was I going half with him for a quarter bag. There was still no drugs going, only heroin. So I said, 'Fuck it.'

I had a pain in my bollocks standing around waiting, so we scored a bag of gear.

We went up to the flat and we split the bag in half on a mirror. He took his half and I watched as he started to cook his gear.

I watched as he put his heroin on a spoon and then put citric on top of that. Then he filled a cup with water, then sucked up the water on the spoon and put the spoon on the ring of the cooker and boiled his gear up.

I was wide-eyed watching all this.

Then he put a filter on the spoon and sucked up his gear. Then he put the spike in a vein in his hand and sent his hit home.

He was out of it and I asked him to do mine, and he did.

I was terrified getting a vein up. I got it up and he got it together. When the gear went in me, it was nicest feeling I ever had. I swear I was really out of it and didn't give a bollocks.

Honestly I can say if the flat collapsed around me, I wouldn't have gave a fuck, the gear was that nice.

But after that I was hooked.

I was sixteen years old. I'm now twenty-nine and I'm still at it. There's no way back. I'll probably die from it.

FAMILY LIFE

YOGI

People think that drugs are a
bad thing, well I suppose
they can be, but I think
its the addiction that
bad. yogi

This is to say thanks
to my mother + father and
family for putting up my
my troubles in the past

'If you don't do something about it, you're not staying in this house!' That was my mother for you. She'd had enough of it. The drugs. The police knocking at the door. The neighbours talking. I think she just done what any loving parent would have done. She couldn't stand around watching her two sons killing themselves from drugs.

'Right! Then I won't be back!'

I remember banging the door shut and walking down the hill at the end of my road thinking, 'Fucking fool. What does she know about drugs.' I thought, 'That's it. I'm not going back to that kip to listen to all that nagging shit. I have my sisters in one ear saying, "Ye dirty junkie bastard. Did you take that money out of my pocket . . . Ma, he's hanging around Meath Street again!" Then my Ma and Da in the other ear, "Show me your arms . . . Show me your eyes . . ."'

I carry on walking and put my hand in my pocket for a cigarette. 'Bollox,' I say to myself, 'I left them in my jacket and that's still in the house, and there's no way I'm going back there to get them. I'll buy some in the shop.'

It was the middle of a beautiful summer's day. Yeah, one of them days for T-shirts and shorts.

I was still thinking of a cigarette when I hear, 'David! David! Will ye wait for fuck sake!' I turned around to see my brother Charles jogging down behind me. I'm thinking, 'The stupid cunt. I betcha he got threw out of the house as well.' That was the thing with me and Charles. He was a year younger than me, and me and him were very close. We done everything together, and when he was in trouble, I was too.

'You're a stupid cunt,' he said.

'What?'

'Why didn't you just say "yeah", you would get off them? She'd have forgot about it in an hour or so.'

'Ah fuck it. I'll go back later on tonight. What's the story with you? Did she tell you to get out as well?'

'No. I told her I'm going to the shop.' Me Ma's a natural worrier. You always have to give her an excuse about where you're going.

'Give us a smoke, will ye, Charles.'

'Yeah, here.'

'I'm going up to Fatima now. What are you doin'?' It was a

stupid question to ask him, because I knew he was going for drugs himself. 'Are ye comin' or what?'

'Yeah, fuck it.'

So we walked on to the main road. I've been livin' near there twenty years and I don't know the name of it now.

'Quick, here's a taxi. Pull him, Charles.'

Charles puts his hand out and the taxi just keeps going by. 'Ye dirty bastard,' he shouts.

That's one thing I hate about taxis. When you're not looking for one, there's loads about, and when you want one, there's none. And there's one going by and the cunt won't even stop for us. They're always on the front page moaning about the hackneys taking the fares. Bunch of juicy wankers.

'Come on,' says Charles, 'we'll get the bus.'

So down we go to the bus stop and within a minute, there's a 50 coming.

'Lovely,' I say to meself as the bus pulls in and we step on.

'Two thirties, please,' Charles says to the driver.

'Where are you going?' asks the driver. He was big and wearing a blue uniform. Like the police.

'The Coombe Hospital.'

'Well, that's fifty-five each.'

'Fuck off, we're only fourteen!'

'Look, it's fifty-five pence, or you're off the bus.'

'Charles, just pay it, will ye.'

'No, me bollox. I'm a school kid.'

'No you're not,' I say to myself. 'You're sixteen, now fucking act it.' In the end, he paid the one pound ten for the two of us.

We went to the back of the bus, grabbing onto the rails, smacking into people as the bus pulled away and making our way to our seat.

At the back of the bus I say, 'Charles, what the fuck were you up to sayin' you were fourteen?'

'Ah, I was only buzzing. Trying to wreck his head,' said Charles laughing. 'Did you see him. He was gettin' freaked out.'

'You're a messing cunt,' I said. He fights with his mouth and can aggravate me. At times I want to turn around and slap him. One time I wanted to slap him that much was when we was thirteen or fourteen and I was out of the house. Him and me Da came lookin' for me. They chased me and I got away from Da, but Charles caught me.

I looked up the front of the bus, looking at the mirror over the driver. I could see his face. He was still fuming.

Four stops later, we were at the Coombe Hospital and as we walked by the driver to get off, Charles just broke his bollox laughing in his face. Ah, I pitied the poor cunt. I think he wanted to get up and punch Charles in the mouth or something.

So off we get and cross the road into a dead-end avenue full of two-bedroom houses. Down the end of it, there's a brick wall about six foot high. So we jumped over that and the first thing we see is two blocks of red brick flats. 'Lovely,' I say to myself. 'There it is. Fatima.'

Fatima is about eight or nine blocks of flats. Each block is named with a letter of the alphabet. And the block I'm looking for is H block. I always thought that was funny. Of all the blocks the dealers pick to sell 'H' from, they would have to pick H Block.

As we're walking over to the flats through one block, I take four twenty-pound notes out of my pocket. 'Charles, have you got a tenner there?'

'Yeah, here.'

I put a twenty back in my pocket thinking to myself, 'There's no way I'm giving a full eighty pounds for the gear.' I'll get ten for seventy.

As soon as we get to the H Block, we're hit from all angles with people selling gear. It's a bit like a market. Instead of, 'Here, I've got lovely shirts here for twenty pound,' the dealer's shouting, 'Are ye looking? Here. He's lovely gear, young fella.'

So Charles sees a bloke he knows who's selling gear at the stairs. But before we get to him, a skinny little bird with the biggest mouth I've heard shouts over, 'Here, young fella. Are ye lookin'? He's lovely gear.'

I just ignore her and walk past.

'Do ye want this gear?'

I swear it's rocket fuel. 'No I don't,' I say, thinking, 'Fucking lying little cunt.' She must have thought we were two fucking fools or something, because I never seen her up here before and if she had nice gear, I would have heard about it, because news travels fast up here in Fatima.

'Here, David. He's nice gear over there,' said Charles.

So over we go to a young fella about seventeen years of age, and he must have weighed about five or six stone. Skinny little fuck. But that's the drugs for you. When you're strung out on heroin, well, heroin is what you have for breakfast, dinner and tea. The only thing food and heroin have in common is the spoon you use for the two of them.

'Awright,' Charles says to the bloke who's selling the gear as we walk over to him. 'Awright, what's the story? When did ye get out?' says Charles.

'The other day.'

'Ah, nice one, you. What's the story? Have you got anything?'

'Yeah. How many do you want?'

'Will you give us four for seventy, will ye?'

'Will ye just watch for the Old Bill? I'm just getting this out.' He goes up the stairs to the landing. It was shady, but you could see old dry piss stains and a couple of ripped plastic sacks some drug dealer was after throwing away. Without a bother he just whips his bags down, holding his breath and squeezing his arse muscles trying to get his fresh batch of gear out. So out it comes. He whips out a hanky. A little wipe. Then straight up to his mouth, bites the bag open and takes four bags out and hands them to Charles.

'There's your money, right,' I say.

'Nice one,' says the dealer.

'Come on. Are ye right, Charles?'

'Yeah.'

'Who's that?' I ask as we walk off.

'Ah, a bloke I was in St Patrick's with. Ah, he's all right. He looked after me when I was in there. Gave me the odd turn on.'

'Do ye know what? You're a dirt bird.'

'Wha?'

'You just threw them bags in your mouth and he just took them out of his arse.'

He just started laughing. He knew I was only buzzing, because when you're walking out of Fatima with a few bags of gear, you're on top of the world. The gear's your pride and joy, and it's what you're living for. And no one is going to take it away . . . the police, the rip-offs, no one.

So a five-minute walk to the shop for a roll of tinfoil, two YOPS,

Mars Bar and Toffee Crisp, ten Blue and two lighters. And a further five-minute walk and we are down at the shack where all the drug addicts meet up for their daily TO and a little chat.

It's amazing the bullshit talk you hear when someone is stoned on gear. And that very person is the very same person that walked by you yesterday with not even a 'hello' to say to you.

So there's me and Charles getting in a window frame without the glass and stepping into a kip of a place that used to be a three-storey office.

The first thing that hits you is the smell of piss and puke. But you don't seem to notice that as you're stepping over holes in the floor. And where there's no holes, you're trying to avoid standing in the shit that someone left there the day before.

'Jaysus, that must have hurt whoever left that there,' Charles said, pointing to a massive big turd on the floor. It must have been about a foot and a half long and two or three inches wide. What you call a proper junkie's shit.

So anyway, we made it through that room without standing in anything and we walk in to the front room and the first thing you notice is that all the floorboards have been ripped up off the beams on the first floor, so you can look straight up to the roof. So we walk through that room and into the hall. Then up to a flight of stairs on the first landing. Then Charles makes a run for it, but all he's running for is the best brick that he can sit on.

'Give us that foil,' he says as he turns a half cement block on its side. He rips a big piece of tinfoil off the roll and covers the top of the brick and then plonks his arse down and I do the same. Then we get to the best bit.

'Give us a lighter, Charles, will ye?'

'Here.'

'Nice one.' I rip a piece of tinfoil about six inches by six inches and a smaller bit about three by three. Then I roll that bit up around a cigarette and put it behind my ear. 'Give us two of them bags, Charles.'

'Yeah, hang on, will ye?'

'Fucking give us them, for fuck sakes!' I shout as he's holding them looking to see which is the biggest. 'Don't take the two biggest ones. Take one and then let me take one!'

'Right. There,' he says, handing me three bags.

So I take the biggest two and give him the last one. I get my piece of tinfoil and put a crease down the left-hand side of it and rest it on my lap, then bite the bag open, shake the powder out of it and pour it onto the foil. Take the pipe from behind my ear, put it in my mouth, strike the lighter, place it under the tinfoil. I put the powder onto the foil and inhale as the powder turns to a liquid form and runs down the foil.

'Lovely,' I say to myself as I light up a cigarette and inhale that and hold my breath for as long as I can to get the best of the heroin. Chasing the heroin, I swallow my saliva a couple time and then exhale.

Me and Charles don't even talk for five minutes until we have a couple of lines into us, because we're enjoying the heroin so much.

'What do you think of the gear, Charles?'

'It's nice.'

'Yeah.'

'So what are you going to do about getting back in the gaff tonight, David?'

'Ah, I'll go over to Linny's.' Linny's my auntie and my mother's closest sister. I'll give her a bit of sweet talk and she'll be on the phone to Ma saying, 'Ah, Annie, leave him. He's trying his best.'

'Sure, David, I'm getting pissed off with this gear. The hassle, the pain. Everything.'

'So am I, Charles.' But I think it's his heroin talking. You're only wanting to get off the gear when you're high.

'Would you go back over to Germany, David?'

'I don't know.'

'It's just Linny was saying to me last week about going over to get off this shit.'

'Here. Give us a smoke over, Charles.'

'What are ye doing? Are ye getting out of here?'

'No, wait. Smoke your other bag.'

'There's no rush. I only told me Ma I was going down to talk to you and that was an hour ago. What are my eyes like? I don't want to get fucked out of the gaff?'

'Ah, well, they're all right.'

A couple of minutes later we're ready to get out of that kip, and we're heading to my Aunt Linny's which is just a couple minutes away. She's in a row of houses and there's a big grotto in the middle of the square.

'Linny! Linny!' I shout as I make my way into her hall.

'Who's that?'

'It's David . . . I hope she's on her own in here,' I said to Charles. 'At least I can have a decent chat and feed her a load of bullshit about how sorry I am and I won't touch it again.'

'Lovely,' I said to myself as I noticed she was on her own. Linny, I have to say, is good-looking for her fifty years. Red-headed.

Me and Charles are sitting down on the two-seater. It's one of them you just sink into. Linny was sitting facing us. I can remember trying in hold my laugh in as she's lecturing us. I don't know how many times she heard these promises before and she still believes in them. It's not that she's a fool, I just think she wants to believe in them. What I loved about Linny, she was always picking up for us after our nanny died in '91.

'David, what are you going to do? Your poor mother, she's broken-hearted over you. And you too, Charles.'

'Linny, she's just paranoid! I swear I'm not touching anything.'

'David, do you think I'm stupid? Look at you. Your eyes are dancing in your head. Your mother is going to have a nervous breakdown. She won't even walk up Meath Street to do her shopping any more. She thinks everyone is talking about her.'

And that's when it kicks in . . . What am I doing to me Ma?

PENNER

I'd been shoplifting for a long time to feed my drug habit. When you're doing it seven days a week, you're bound to get caught the odd time.

I'm back in Mountjoy and just over my heroin withdrawal sickness. I'm in a single cell and can't believe the peace and tranquillity. Outside I was killing myself slowly on gear, but now I'm clean and feel as if I've been reborn. Heroin stripped me of my emotions, my personality, my sex drive – even my love of music. But now I'm laughing and singing in my cell every night, even though the woman I love is with another man.

Marie was fourteen and I was seventeen when we met. She was my wife and partner for twenty years, the mother of my two children. She never stopped loving me, she just couldn't live with my drug habit any more.

Marie had the patience of an angel. One day in particular, I told her I was going to stay in bed and try and go cold turkey. I thought I'd be strong enough to suffer three days of withdrawals. She couldn't do enough. Breakfast, dinner and tea in bed. Even though I'd lost me appetite, she fussed over me and tried to coax me to eat. She went to the village shops and bought me some music magazines and a large bottle of Irish whiskey. 'There ye are, love,' she said. 'That might help you sleep.' I didn't have the heart to tell her that I would be twice as bad the next day, whether I drank the whiskey or not. And I drank the whole bottle.

Next morning, when Marie brought Aine and Aoife to school, I dressed quickly and legged it out to get drugs. I just couldn't do it, even for her and the kids. I was losing her, but I felt helpless.

Marie wasn't stupid. Some of my family and friends had already died by catching the virus through infected needles. She knew that because of me, I could put her health in danger as well as her unborn children. When I was desperate or sick and without my own works, I'd used numerous times throughout the years after other addicts. You just don't think about the virus or AIDS when you're craving for a fix to stop the hurt. Well, I didn't anyway.

This time, I thought, I might stand a chance if I could prove how much I still really loved and wanted her. A clean bill of health from me would ease her fears. It might change her mind about me, so I started a last-ditch attempt to win her back and turn my whole sad life around.

I dropped in to see the doctor and told him I'd like an HIV test.

I'd been on heroin for most of eighteen years and never wanted to know or cared whether I had the virus or not. Life was a game of chance, luck and heroin. But now whereas I wasn't afraid of getting the virus or dying, I was afraid I'd get a positive result that would wipe out my last hope of getting my wife back.

I was up in the school doing Leaving Cert English when I was interrupted by an officer who told me I had a visit. On the way down the stairs to the main prison, I was wondering who it could be. When I reached the gate, I saw a screw with handcuffs. 'Are ye looking for me?' I said.

He looked like he wished he was somewhere else. No one likes escorting drug addicts. He looked like a prisoner in uniform. Black hair, cut tight. Moustache and goatee beard, and a tiny scar, like a crescent moon, above his left eyebrow. He was a lot younger than me and smaller than my five foot ten inches.

'You're goin' to the hospital.' He spoke in a deep Dublin brogue. 'Follow me.'

He took me down to reception and told me to strip. This was to make sure I had no weapons to aid an escape. 'I don't want to escape,' I said. 'Yez were tryin' to throw me out last month, and I wouldn't go.'

'It makes me no odds. Rules are rules.'

It made no odds to me either way. When you've been on heroin as long as I've been, strip searches are frequent. It didn't bother me at all. Between the drugs squad, the garda and the screws, they'd probably seen me naked more times than my own wife.

I stripped down to my jocks and threw my clothes on the table in front of me. I stripped quickly, so that he'd have to search quickly. As I was clean and feeling good, I stared at him throughout the search. He looked ill at ease and embarrassed. After lowering my jocks for him, he searched them and didn't look me in the eye once. I was dressed again in minutes.

At the main gate, two more screws joined us. It was about 11.30 a.m. and the sun was shining.

Prison to hospital is five minutes. I walked across the main road to the hospital escorted by three screws who had me in cuffs and led me with a long chain. It was very embarrassing. We passed the women's prison on the way. It made me think of Brendan Behan singing, 'And I wished it was where I dwelled.' I felt quietly

70

contented to be out in the street again, a VIP with these three walking alongside. I also felt like a murderer. The main road was busy with lunchtime traffic and I wondered what people were thinking as they stared from cars, buses and lorries.

We got to the hospital waiting room and sat down. A little boy of about eight or nine sat facing me with his mother. He stared at the chains and handcuffs. When I caught his eye, I gave him my best smile and wondered what he thought of me. I wanted to lift up my handcuffed fist high in the air and say, 'It's disgraceful the way they treat you for robbing a few CDs, isn't it?'

I wished I could be his age again.

As I sat down in the surgery chair, it was for Marie really. I knew I wasn't getting this blood test for me. I knew I must get a negative result as the matronly nurse probed my forearm for a healthy vein. 'Nurse, I don't think you'll find a vein there. I used them all up. You might find one on my shoulder near my neck.' There was a nice clean hospital smell off her. Starch and antiseptic. She wasn't fat, just pleasantly plump.

'Let's have a look anyway.'

'That's the first needle that's went into my arm with no heroin in it in five or six years,' I think. 'She's wasting her time. I've often spent half an hour in tears trying to find a vein on that arm.'

She felt for a vein beside the mainline in the crook of my right arm. 'Now, Michael, see, miracles do happen,' she said as she loosened the elasticated tourniquet. I was surprised. My blood looked dark crimson and black as it trickled into the syringe.

'Sister, can you mark my sample "confidential", please?'

'They're all confidential.'

'No, Sister, a certain officer took a friend of mine's results off the medical tray in the prison and opened it and read it before handing it to him.'

'Well, we send them away, so it's out of our hands. See the Governor.'

'Okay, thanks.'

During those ten days that I had to wait for my results, I went through a lot of soul searching. Did I really want to know the results? Would it make any difference to Marie or not? Would I throw caution to the wind if I had the virus? If it's positive, would it make me develop a worse habit when I'm released? It would be like a death sentence. I wanted to know. But I didn't want to know.

During this I had a surprise visit from her. I was thrilled, because I hadn't seen her since before I got locked up about four months ago.

Her long blonde hair was even longer than the last time I saw her. It was freshly washed. She wore narrow black trousers and the usual black leather ankle boots with stiletto heels. As she got closer, I thought, 'Her new man doesn't know how lucky he is.' Even though I fucked up, I still loved her.

I sat halfway down in the visit room. A screw on a high chair sat on each end, about forty feet apart. I was separated from Marie by a four-foot-wide counter. An eighteen-inch-high perspex partition ran down the middle. There were visitors and prisoners there already. Most of them leaned on the counter with folded arms, chins resting on the partition. The new cameras cover every angle. Big Brother was peeping.

I leaned over and kissed her before she sat down. She looked pale and wasn't smiling like usual.

'How' ya, Marie. You're lookin' well.'

She only half smiled. 'So are you. You're putting on some weight.'

'I'm strung out on the rice now, that's all.'

'It's well for ye.'

'Did the kids get me letters? And did you get the poems I sent?' Aine was our eldest daughter. She was blonde and pretty like her mother and had just turned eighteen. Aoife was just fifteen and more like me. I think I treated her too much like the son I'd never had. When she was younger, we'd go catching frogs and newts. I sent them a letter and a poem at least every two weeks.

'Yeah, they're lovely. Your eldest is working now.' She was doing an office-procedures course and was still living at home. 'She's going to type your next letter.'

'Ah, sure! That's great. I can't wait to hear from them. By the way, I went for an HIV test. I've to wait for the results.' I could hear children all around us in the visiting room. They were laughing and playing. Marie raised her eyebrows waiting for me to say more. When we were still together, she'd asked me to have one, but I'd never got around to it. There was a silence then as I looked into her eyes.

Marie said, 'I've had an HIV test myself.' I could smell her perfume.

'What made you go for that?'

'I'm pregnant.'

I felt like someone had given me a hard clatter in the face. 'You're not serious, Marie? You're pregnant?' I thought I was hearing things. This was one of my worst fears. I was gutted. The final nail ran into my heart as I looked at her. She's only after becoming a granny, how could she. 'You must be mad,' I said. 'There's Aine's baby in the house already.'

'I'm due next February. I didn't plan it.'

I had a million things I wanted to say, but they went out of my mind. So that's it, I thought, that's why she's not her usual bubbly self.

'Do you want to see a scan of the baby?'

'Yeah. Give us a look.' The black and white picture shows the baby's features. 'That's a big baby,' I say when she puts the picture back into her bag. 'I hope you don't mind all the poems I'm sending you, Marie. I'm not trying to get into your head or anything . . .'

'You know I don't mind. I love getting them.'

I thought to meself, 'At least she's leaving me a bit of hope. I wouldn't care if she had twins. Or even fuckin' triplets. I'd still love her.'

Something definitely died inside me that day. Having another man's baby, mistake or no mistake, was not what I wanted to hear. Thank God, I was strong enough to handle it.

If she'd told me two or three months earlier, I would have thought very hard about ending it all one way or another, because my mind was so fragile.

At least she told me face to face. All I could do was congratulate her.

The following week went in a haze, until the morning my test result was due. At breakfast, I peered over the rail at the top of the wing. I could look down to the medics tray below. I couldn't see any envelopes or letters. I had a bad feeling that I was going to get a positive. This was my karma again for all the pain and heartache I'd caused Marie. She's pregnant for another man, gone forever, and I'm dying slowly with the HIV virus. It was only what I deserved.

Dinner time and tea time came and went quickly. There was still no letter for me on the medics tray. I steeled myself by walking around the yard for nearly two hours. At supper time before lock-up, I approached the medic. 'Mr Curly?' I said.

'Yes, Mick, what can I do ye for?'

'I was supposed to get blood test results back today.'

'Oh, yes! "Michael Penrose". The letter is down in the base. Ye got a negative.'

'Lovely,' I said. 'Just what I wanted.'

'Do ye want a photocopy, Mick?'

'Ah, sure. Why not! I can frame it and stick it on me cell wall.' I felt joy and relief as I climbed the stairs back up to my cell, but as soon as I saw Marie's picture in front of me, I was dejected and depressed.

The pain of cold turkey was child's play compared to the heartache I was going through now.

BRIE

You alone can do it, but you
cannot do it alone.

Brie

If I start naming names, I'll forget some-one, so I just want to say 'thanks' to everyone!!! Special thank's to Martha, who helped me believe in my self.

Brie

I don't know who got more of a shock, me or Louise Kelly, a copper who had a warrant for me. Around the corner and straight into her. No point in running. Her six-foot-two-inch sidekick would of had all seven and a half stone of me down like a light. So there I stood. Mouth open. Words failing me. Heart thumping like crazy. Weak at the knees, thinking, 'Oh, my God, I'm fucked.'

No need for handcuffs. Just one look at my emaciated, run-down, strung-out body told her I was in no state to do a runner. There were few words spoken between us, but the most memorable were the ones uttered into her walkie-talkie. 'Car requested to Temple Bar for transportation of prisoner back to Pearse Street.'

I stuck my hands in my pockets and sighed.

It was January 8th. A calm, crisp, clear night, way past midnight. I told myself to have a good look around 'cause it would be a long time before I tasted freedom again. There's never a guard around when you need one, but there was no shortage of them this night.

Just my luck. The driver of the squad car that pulled up was a cheeky bastard that I'd known too long from around town. I ignored his smart comments all the way back to Pearse Street, as I was more interested in catching the last glimpses of civilisation as the car sped up Dame Street. The pubs weren't long shut . . . Couples arm in arm, and everybody suddenly seemed to me to be having a great time . . . Past two of my favourite old haunts; the twenty-four-hour Spar shop and the Central Bank, I just felt like crying.

I knew the drill. Not as if I hadn't been nicked before. But this time at Pearse Street Gard Station something was different. I knew I wasn't going to talk my way out of this one. That sinking feeling with me since the chance encounter with Louise Kelly had sunk, leaving me lost.

I was marched up to the desk sergeant's counter. It was late at night, but it was still a hive of activity. Someone shouted out, 'All right, Bernadette, nicked at last!'

I looked through the counter. All I could see was loads of blue uniforms, sitting at desks. Shuffling papers and drinking coffee.

The desk sergeant was another familiar face. A grey-haired fatherly type that I'm sure was thanking his lucky stars I was no daughter of his. 'Any distinguishing scars or tattoos?'

Same old bullshit. In no humour to try and be smart, I shook my head.

'Height?' he asked.

My smartness returning, I ventured, 'I guess you're about six feet.'

I asked for a doctor; first thing all junkies do when they get nicked.

The desk sergeant smiled. Not a ha-ha sort of smile. More an evil grin. 'Why? Are you sick?'

'No. I'm a drug addict,' I replied sweetly, gritting my teeth and knowing if I got smart my chances of getting a doctor would be halved. The bit he didn't hear me mutter was, 'As if ye didn't know, ye fat fuck.'

Next on the list, the strip search.

For anyone who's never had one, it's an undignified process, but you get used to it fairly quickly. It's one of the things that come hand in hand with being a drug addict. There were two female officers wearing rubber gloves. I was freezing cold and wanted to get it over with quick as possible. I'd nothing to hide except my dignity, but I whipped my clothes off.

Surveying my possessions on the table, I realised I had no hair brush, I had no cigarettes, and I was fifteen pence short of the price of ten. On the brighter side, I had half a packet of Polos and a Kinder Surprise toy.

Finally, the search over, I was put into a cell. I knew I had a long night ahead of me. I was disgusted to find the cell was spotlessly clean. No graffiti to amuse myself reading. (Thinking back over the years, a lot of the best stuff I've ever read has been on the back of toilet doors and police station cell walls.)

Suddenly a voice jolted me back to reality.

'Take the laces out or the runners off altogether, Bernadette.' I weighed my options. Okay, I could freeze with my runners off or spend twenty minutes unlacing them. I opted for the latter.

Time to check out the rubber mattress and blanket. My excuse for a bed. I hesitantly examined the blanket. Pink cotton on one side, horse hair on the other. I was trying not to think of the numerous people that had occupied this cell before me and what they could have done on my blanket . . . 'Okay, doing well so far. No major stains. Just a few spots of blood.' Even more hesitantly, I sniffed it. Surprisingly it didn't stink.

With that done, I sat down and wondered how the fuck was I going to occupy my mind for the next ten hours. The feeling of despair and helplessness was unreal. I mentally made a note never to commit a crime again. Well, good advice under the circumstances. A bit late though.

I spent the next hour or so going through all the ifs and buts. If I had of listened to Joey and went straight back to the B&B, if I hadn't been so cocky, walking around the very area that the coppers had warrants out for me: most of them knowing me nearly as well as my own Ma. Some of them even better.

The last conversation I'd had with Joey before I got nicked, I confessed that I'd taken the next day's phy before I came out that night. He gave me a bollocking for that . . . Maybe it was fate. If I hadn't of, I'd be dying sick right now . . . Then, the other side of the coin, by keeping it, I'd be in bed in the B&B now.

Nothing to do except think.

Boredom sets in very quickly when you're on your own in a cell. You end up counting everything from the spots on the wall to track marks on your arms. All that can be heard is coppers laughing and the jangling of keys, both of which have to be the most annoying noises ever. Four Polo mints later, a lot of thinking, a lot more tears and even a few press-ups – as I said, anything to keep ye amused – the keys rattled again.

Door flies open and the question, 'Burger King or Abracadabra?' put to rest my hope that this might be the doctor. Nah, just the fucking waiter . . . Food being the last thing on my mind. Chancing my arm, I asked for a cup of tea and a cigarette.

Without replying the copper slammed the door. Was this the way of saying 'no', I wondered? Whatever charm school they sent him to was a waste of fucking money.

Stretching back on my bed, I started on my nails. I was saving them till I got really bored. Somewhere about nail six, my waiter was back with a cup of tea and a cigarette. I could have kissed him. The fact that he was a copper stopped me.

Typical. Sugar in the tea.

If you asked for sugar you wouldn't get it. I wasn't in the position to be fussy, so I drank it, the cigarette, only heaven.

KING

I am sick and tired of, not
been there for them. and I mean
I am going to start been a rally
good falter to. them.

So I ~~haven't~~ got much more
to say only I love and miss them so much.

Love

Paddy

My son Lee, he is two years of age. He has a lovely big, bright and friendly smile. He has lovely big blue eyes. He also has lovely blond hair. He is also a very fat and chubby little bollox who I love so much and adore with all my heart.

He was such a good child when he was growing up. He is so good at sleeping and eating his food. If I can remember, I don't think he had many sleepless nights, but even if he had of had, I would have known . . . His mother, Angie, would have made sure I got up to attend his every cry. But also she is a great mother and I don't know where she gets her patience from. (Well, I know if I was after bringing up five kids, I would have been in DunDrum Mental Hospital by now.)

My son Lee has a great temperament, but he can also be bold at times.

The thing that really gets to me is Christmas time. It's when I'm not there to see Lee and the other kids open their presents. It is such a happy time for me. Just seeing their big and smiling faces. God, it makes my heart bleed. But I am willing to make a go at being there for him next year and many years down the road.

My son means so much to me and his mother. He is the apple of my eye and his mother's. He is such a cute little lad, and lovable and huggable. You would just die for him. Well, I know I would. He is so important to me.

So is my little girl Jodie. She is seven years old and has so much in common with Lee. She also has lovely blond hair. And I love her and adore her as much as Lee. They mean so much to me, it's unbearable.

I am sick and tired of not being there for them, and I mean I am going to start being a really good father to them. I love them and miss them so much.

KENNO

I hope the young
People of today might
in some way learn
some thing from this
Story!!

Dedicate this to My
Granmother and in
Rememberance of My
Mother and Fatther

Kenno!!

The saddest point in my life was when my mother and father died: I was sixteen when my mother died and was serving an eight-year sentence which made it a lot worse because I was locked up when given the bad news.

I can remember as clear as yesterday.

It was a Friday afternoon. I was only after coming from the gym. I left early as I was expecting a visit from my mom and I wanted to have my shower and get cleaned up. So after that I made my way up on the landing I was on in St Patrick's. I remember I was buzzin' around having a laugh with a few of the blokes on the wing when out of the blue I was called by the prison chaplain.

My first thought was, 'He's looking to tell me about the phone call I had previously asked him that morning to make for me.' So thinking nothing of it, I walked up and asked him did he make the call. But he just nodded and said, 'Oh there you are. I've been all over the place looking for you! Hang on a sec, I'll be with you in a minute.' And he just turned around and started talking to another inmate.

So anyway, I went over and sat on a table to roll a smoke thinking to myself, 'It's probably about my mam. She's still a bit sick and won't be able to make it up as she had been ill for the week or so beforehand with bad headaches but had recovered and was in good health and had promised to be in to visit me no matter what.' So my first thought was that she had fell ill again and wouldn't be able to make it in to see me!

So then the priest calls me and says, 'I want to speak to you about your mother.'

So I followed him to his office, went in and sat down on a chair facing a window overlooking the prison yard. It was a miserable day. The rain was pelting down against the window when suddenly he broke the news and told me my mother had passed away at quarter to seven that morning due to an AIDS-related illness she had been suffering from due to being a chronic drug addict. She was thirty-four years of age.

That news was like a four-hundred-pound sledgehammer hitting me straight in the face. That's really the only way I can express my feelings on paper in words.

I don't really know how to talk about how I feel, so a lot of my feelings I keep bottled up I guess.

I was released to attend my mother's funeral on 19 January 1995 for one week. Given five pounds at the gate. In other words told not to spend it all in the one shop and to behave myself while I was out. (The pack of bastards have no heart, respect or remorse. That's something I'll leave for another day . . .)

With my pockets full of money, I walked into town in a daze; the realisation of what had happened creeping up on me the whole time.

I got the Dart to Killiney train station, got off and just walked aimlessly around as it was the first time since the news was broken that I had time to think and my own privacy. I guess I needed time before going home and facing my family which was the worst part.

My head was fucked up! When I finally went home, to be honest, I can't remember much of that day, as before I even went to the house, I got a few bags of H to block everything out . . . It was just too much to deal with sober.

After the funeral I went down and bought two plane tickets to London for me and my girlfriend, as I was under no circumstances going back to prison.

Me and my girlfriend went to London the day I was due back in prison. My destination was Brixton where my father was living in a squat.

He was unable to return home for the funeral, because he had warrants out for his arrest due to the armed robberies he had done the previous year.

So anyway, me and the girl I was with arrived in Brixton.

We hadn't got a clue where the fuck we were going or how to find my Da's flat . . . We found it eventually anyway.

I never mentioned before, I don't think, that my father also suffered from HIV and was a drug addict.

So when we finally got inside the flat, his girlfriend who's also a drug addict and suffers from AIDS answered the door.

We said our hellos and she directed me into the sitting room where my Da was and said her and my girlfriend would be in in a minute.

I don't really know how to explain this but what I seen sitting in a filthy armchair beside the window did not look one bit like the father I knew. At thirty-three years of age, he looked like an old man. His clothes were dirty and torn, his hair was long, he had a full beard, and he had withered away to about seven and a half stone.

He had got strung out on crack cocaine.

I can't even try to explain the pain I felt inside from only after burying my mother and then to come over and see my Da like this. It broke me heart. It wasn't him. It wasn't the father I once knew. As much as the heroin did, the crack really tore him apart.

There was no food in the presses . . . My two little half-brothers were also sick with having to enter into the world with the AIDS virus too. But to make matters worse, they were starving.

To cut a long story short, that's when I started going out pulling off robberies trying to get money desperately to feed my brothers with food.

My dad and his girl with crack, and me and my girl, it was just too much. I had to come home. So as soon as I got the money, I packed my bags without even saying a goodbye and that was the last time I ever seen my dad alive.

I lasted three weeks in England and two weeks when I came home before I was caught to serve out the rest of my sentence.

My girlfriend didn't wait around for long. She found someone else and vanished. So once again I was on my own. Just waiting to be hit with the rest of the bad news!

When the first person in your life dies, it takes months of heart-break to get over. But now so many people that were close to me have died, nothing shocks or sets me up any more. I've seen almost everything there is to see. And have felt almost everything there is to feel.

Only a few months had passed since my mother died until I was in the situation all over again. Only this time my father had passed away from some sort of heart failure called cardio-biograph but it was also AIDS-related. He died on 29 August 1996, aged thirty-four years.

Since that day I think all sense of feelings had vanished from me, because I feel empty inside.

THE SCORE

GOTZY

"Wisdom is the principle thing,
therefore get wisdom,
and in all your getting,
get understanding."

For Family & friends
inlaws & out laws

Gotzy

I've got the bed covers pulled right up as far as my face. It's fuckin' freezing. Anita is still asleep right beside me. I don't want to wake her. Not yet anyways. It must be eight in the morning. I don't think it could be much more than eight. I am wide awake, lying here just thinking over lots and lots of things. I have lots I need to think about.

I am in my mother's house. I have not stayed in this house in a long time. Looking at this small room around me, I pick out all the things that are new. It's all different from how it used to be. I think of the cold again. The temperature is definitely one thing that's not changed in this room. It's like a bleedin' fridge.

I hate being cold.

I have a busy day ahead. Well, maybe eventful would be a better word. One particular event being the reason I stayed here last night: I am supposed to be going away today. I am not happy about it. (Ain't nobody else I know happy about it neither.) I lie here thinking . . . trying to come up with some excuse for putting off going away. I can't find one and there is no reason trying. I'll end up going in the end, no matter what I do. I can't change that. It's a catch twenty-two situation, and I lose both ways.

Still, I keep on thinking. I think about how long I could be gone for. I got no answer to that. Just guesses.

At ten-thirty I am supposed to be in Dublin Circuit Court. I expect to go away for a while. A good while. Doing a bunk is a choice. I done one already. But there ain't no point this time. It would just guarantee me a longer stay in the Joy. Get it done and finished with is what I think.

Fuck it. I will just hope for the best. Yeah, fuck it.

Something inside me is tired. Tired and wants me to go away.

Inside I am fed up and tired.

Going away would be a break. It would nearly be a holiday from where I am now. Everything around me seems to be drugs money drugs drugs drugs and more drugs. I feel like I know nothin' else. No time for nothin' else. No choice to do anything else. Even now the day's already got its edge. I am sick. I am if I think I am. I am so used to beginning my day sick. It's what I'm used to. I think I sometimes feel sick just out of routine. I expect to be sick so I am sick.

Sick is the excuse to do my gear now rather than later.

I have some gear. It's underneath my bed calling me.

It's already cooked and ready for me.

I want it but I don't want to move to get it. I don't want to wake Anita by moving. I want a few more minutes to think.

My gear is a distraction while I think. It calls me. I keep thinking that it's there.

I think about David and Dean, my two boys. I will miss them when I go. I hope and wonder will they miss me? I don't want to keep thinking of them right now. I'll find a thousand regrets about things I didn't or did do. Things I meant to do. What they missed out on. What they will miss out on when I go. All those people I care about. People who don't want me going no place but don't want me stayin' neither. Stayin' so I keep livin' the same shit over and over like I have been doing.

This morning is different for me. I have never turned up in a court to get sent down. I have never been sure of the big sentence I expect today. I still have the choice of doing a bunk on it. But I think that's just a choice between a big sentence and a fuckin' bigger one.

That gear is still there.

Do a bunk or go to court? It's a simple choice that ain't so simple . . . Fuck it. Two words. Fuck it. I will go to court as planned. Get it done with.

Why do I say 'fuck it'?

I think about it.

I say fuck it about lots of decisions I got to make. It's a good answer. A good answer when you're a junkie. It's a quick decision. It's a laid-back answer for everything.

That gear is calling me again. That's why I decided, fuck it. Any other decision's gonna take longer. I don't want to wait any more for my gear. My gear won't wait any more for me.

My clothes are on the floor. I pull them over to me and dress myself. I try to keep it as quiet as I can. Anita wakes up anyway. We share the gear between the two of us. The first turn on of the day. The best one of the day. The first always is.

Now I have some things I have to do. I have to get ready for today. Make sure I have anything I need with me, i.e. drugs and more drugs.

I spent yesterday shopping. Shopping for drugs and the bits that go with them. It was a poxy day. Fuckin' cold, wet and busy. In the morning me and Anita went to Ballyier to get gear and napps. Heroin and morphine tablets. I would need as many as I could get to stop me getting sick when I go away. We had to wait around in the cold to get them. Most of the time you have to wait. That's the worst part. Standin' in the pissin' rain . . . cold. Then we scored.

We scored twenty tablets, and since it was such a pain waiting, we done the only thing a junkie can do – fuck off to the nearest field or some place quiet to make the waiting worth while. Off we went for a turn on. I love it when I'm able to make a beeline for a turn on.

We went down behind a school, and to the end of a field behind it. Right down to the end to the corner of the field where the wall surrounds it. Mucky and wet, no problem. A junkie can make himself at home any place he has to take his gear.

I got my spoon, lighter and water out. I put my works beside me. I crushed four tablets on the spoon. I was in a hurry. I always am at a time like this. Waiting is the worst. I sucked the water into the works and squirted it onto the spoon. I gave Anita the lighter to hold under the spoon. The bastard kept blowing out with the wind. I knelt down and moved closer to the corner for shelter. Carefully so I didn't spill what's on the spoon.

No sooner had we started than we had to stop. This fuckin' stupid horse that was in the field decides to wander on down to us. He wasn't fuckin' shy or nothin'. Right the fuckin' way up he comes. I thought, 'Fuck this horse.'

But Anita said, 'Ah, get him away,' and gets all nervous and shit. Fuckin' women. What the fuck could I do? I was holding a full spoon. (This sort of shit pisses me off.) Fuck off, the bleedin' horse. Fuck off, Anita. Fuck's bleedin' sakes.

I got the spoon down safely to the ground, got rid of the horse and went back to what I was doing, shouting at Anita while I was at it.

Third attempt. I tried and tried and tried. The lighter she's holdin' kept blowin' out. It's always the same. 'Gimme the fuckin' lighter,' I said. I bit the steel guard off it, turned the little thing for adjusting the gas, and put the guard back on.

'Now it won't go fuckin' out now. Light it . . . Hold it! Put it under the spoon. Simple,' I says. 'Good . . .'

Then Whoosh!

'Jesus H. Bleedin' Christ!' The fuckin' flame on the lighter was turned up, all right. Right the way fuckin' up. And what does the woman go and do? Jumps and knocks me fuckin' spoon over.

I didn't say a fuckin' word. I was going to snap.

I think I is definitely turning up in court. The longer I get away the better.

BOO-BOO

I would like to thank MARSHA HUNT for all her
help and advice and for giving me this opportunity
to do something I enjoyed. THANKS.

BOO-BOO.

This short story is dedicated to my son — Boo-Boo Junior, for him to read when he is older.

I'm in the pub with my girlfriend Claire and her brother Brian. It's early in the afternoon, so there's only a few of the locals scattered around. My Da is sitting at the bar glued to the horseracing on the telly. There is an old guy sitting near him, muttering to himself about how his horse should have won. He's still got the cream of his pint of Guinness on his upper lip.

A little old lad is at the cigarette machine, cursing it because he can't get his smokes out.

Brian sticks another fifty pence in the pool table for another game, while I go up and order another round of drinks.

Claire is twenty-three. Only five years older than me. What I really like about her is that she's got a great personality. She knows how to have a buzz. She has gone into the toilet to do a pregnancy test. I had to fork out twelve quid for it. I didn't mind the money, but I coulda got somebody to do it for a fiver.

I'm about to smash into the balls when the phone rings. I'm waiting for a call to let me know if there is a bit of work going down tonight. The call is not for me, so I get back to my game of pool.

All of a sudden, BANG! It hits me and I think, 'Fuck me, I could be a dad soon!' I have a hundred different thoughts running around in my head . . . If she comes out and tells me she isn't pregnant, I know I'd be disappointed. But at the same time, I wonder if I'm ready to be a dad. At the moment I'm nothing but a junkie and have been for the last few years.

How can I be a decent father if I can't stop taking heroin?

I'm brought back to reality by the noise of the phone ringing. Then the barman gives me a shout to tell me it's for me.

I pick up the phone and say, 'Yeah, what's happening?'

The voice at the other end says, 'Yeah, John here. How ye keepin'?'

We get into some small talk for a minute until I ask, 'What's doin' for tonight?'

He tells me he's got something happening and says he's got everything sorted.

I ask if it's the jeweller's or the restaurant. Which one are we robbin'?

'It's the restaurant,' he tells me.

We arrange a time and place to meet and hang up.

The jukebox is on and Bob Dylan is singing a song about his

tambourine man which I find ironic, because I was just thinking of ringing my own tambourine man. That's when I see Claire coming out of the toilet. I see her face and I know exactly what she is going to say to me. Tears coming out of her eyes. She hands me the kit.

I'm lookin' at it and saying, 'Yeah? What the fuck does this mean?'

She sits down and tells me she is pregnant. A great shout of happiness escapes through my lips. I feel over the moon, on top of the world, and nothing on this earth can ever take that moment away from me.

I go out to the bar to my Da and buy him a drink and bring him into the pool room to give him the good news. I sit him down and say, 'I've got some news for ye.'

He says, 'What? Youse got engaged?'

I tell him, 'No. You're going to be a grandad.'

He shakes my hand and congratulates us.

I start thinking about my tambourine man again and think, 'Fuck it, it's time to celebrate.'

And I go over and make a phone call. I've got to meet him in half an hour.

The four of us are in a good mood, having a buzz and playing pool when my Ma comes in. She asks, 'What are youse all so cheerful about?'

I tell her to sit down and ask her what she wants to drink. But she won't have a drink. It's too early in the day. I persuade her to have a glass of orange.

So we tell her the good news.

And she said she thought it was something like that. She is over the moon about it as she's giving Claire big hugs and kisses.

They're all sitting around laughing and joking. All I'm thinking about at the moment is how quick this hour is going to pass. Fuck it, I'm getting outta here.

I pull Claire aside and tell her I have to meet someone.

'Who is it?' she asks.

So I jokingly tell her it's a nice-looking blond. She laughs at the joke while pretending to give me a clatter.

I lie and tell her it's John.

'So I take it you'll be going out tonight?'

'Yeah, I got a bit of work on for later.'

'Work! That's not work. Anyway, you can't keep this up now. You've got responsibility now.'

'Ah look! Don't be getting into me head about this, I need some bleeding money.'

'And you have to start getting off that gear before . . .'

I cut her off in mid-sentence and tell her I'll talk to her later; and tell her I'll meet her in my Ma's in a couple of hours, wave my goodbyes to the rest of them and run out the door.

It's about half two and I've got about twenty minutes to kill before meeting Mr Tambourine Man. I've got to meet him in the shopping centre. 'Fuck it, I'll go up now and hang around for a bit.'

Walking up the town and the place is buzzing. Everyone seems to be running around like headless chickens. I'm going by the chipper and get a whiff of food being cooked. 'I'll get a bag of chips, 'cause I won't be able to eat much if I get too stoned.' And I feel like getting too stoned.

I do a U-turn into the chipper and I'm surprised to see there isn't a queue. Big-Bird is on behind the counter. He's a seven-foot-two lanky streak of misery of Italian breed. He's an all right bloke. He sees me and says in this Italian accent, ''Ello, Bobby. Ow you do in fight the udder night? I see 'im come hit you with a stick, but you hit 'im back and take stick off 'im and he run away with you chasing 'im.'

'No man, I haven't seen him since. But he's going to wake up smashed up when I get me hands on the cunt. I'll shove a fucking stick up his fucking arse and have him shitting splinters for a bleeding week.'

Me chips are done, so he sticks them in the bag and pours on plenty of salt and vinegar, just the way I like them. I give him eighty pence and fuck off.

The shopping centre is about a hundred feet ahead of me on the opposite side of the road. As usual, I just walk across the road so the cars will have to stop. About halfway across, some baldy elder lemon starts beeping his horn. Throwing a chip at his windscreen, I shout, 'Fuck off ye baldy prick!' I can see him waving his fist at me.

Ha! Ha! I get a buzz annoying people like him.

'Bobby!'

I hear someone calling me and turn around, and I see Mr

Tambourine Man coming towards me. He's about six foot. A good-lookin' bloke, not that I'm that way inclined, mind you. I have to look up at him when I'm talking.

'Awright Anto, what's happening?'

'Ah, ye know yerself, same ol' shit. Giz a chip.'

'Fuck off and buy your own.'

'Fuck off,' he says while putting his hand in the bag. 'I heard you were fighting again the other night.'

'What do ye mean "again"? That's the first scrap I've had in ages. Anyway, it wasn't much of a scrap. The shite-bag legged it . . . Have you got any gear on ye?'

'I only have a few bags on me.' He talks with that slow slur you get when you're on the smack for a while. 'What are ye looking for anyway?'

'Give us five bags for eighty pound!'

'Yeah, all right. Are ye coming for a turn on?'

'Yeah. Where're we going?' We were outside the shoe shop. It was about three o'clock.

'Well, I have to go up to me flat to get your gear, so we might as well go up there. Me bird's not in. She's gone to see her sister in Cherry Orchard. She has the jaundice.'

His flat is only up the road, so we get there in a few minutes. It's a basement flat in a three-storey gaff. Not a bad place. It's got one bedroom, small bathroom and kitchen and a decent sized sitting-room.

We get right to work.

'Anto, have ye got any citric?'

'No. I have a lemon in the fridge.' He goes out the back to get the smack and I sit down, getting my gizmo ready.

He hands me eight Qs and tells me to pick five. I just grab any five of them and give him back the other three. 'What's this gear like?'

'It's not the worst. But it's not the best either.' He gives me a spoon.

I put three Qs on and a drop of lemon, get me filter and me one mil ready for action. And start cooking.

I hate the smell of gear getting cooked.

I'm sucking the gear up off the spoon and Anto is only starting to put a light to his spoon.

'Giz a tourniquet, Anto.'

'There's one in the drawer under the telly.'

MTV is on but the sound's turned down. He is standing over beside the kitchen when I say, 'I have me bird up the stick.'

'Well then, I think congratulations are in order.'

'Ah, don't start that shit as well.'

'When did you find out?'

'Just a while ago. Now shut up till I get this into me.'

'At least we can't say you're shooting blanks any more.'

'Me bleedin' veins are fucked, Anto.'

'Try your hand.'

'Where the fuck you think I'm trying. Me fucking flute!'

'You're always giving out about your veins,' he says as he's pushing his gear into him. 'Do ye want me to get that for ye?' he asks while cleaning his gizmo out.

'Fuck off. I have it now.' As I send the smack home, I get the same old feeling, a little rush through the body. 'This gear's fucking shit.'

'Ye can't get decent gear in this fuckin' country.'

'Have ye any phy there, Anto?'

'I only have four or five hundred mils.'

'Sell us a hundred, will ye?'

'Yeah, all right. Are ye drinking it now?' he asks as he takes the bottle out from under a drawer.

'Yeah. I'll roll a joint.' He gives me the phy in a plastic container. 'I hate the taste of this shit.'

'Ah, just hold your nose and swallow it.'

I do just that. The liquid hits my stomach and I start dry retching. The tears are rolling down my face. 'Have ye much gear left, Anto?'

'I've about twenty quarters.'

'Give us another three. I'll pay ye in the morning.'

'Fuck off. Ye have money in yer pocket.'

'I've only about thirty pound and I need it, 'cause I'm going off tonight.'

'I need the money off ye tomorrow.'

'Yeah. I'll fucking pay ye! Have ye any foil? I'm going to smoke one of these.'

'Yeah. I think I'll have a smoke meself. So what are ye gonna do now with yer bird up the stick?'

'I don't know. Try to knock this shit on the head first. And I got charged the other night for some gaff in Killiney.'

'Yeah. I heard something about that. What happened?'

'Ah, the fuckin' jackass I was with opened the bleedin' window and set the alarm off. After me telling him don't open any windows or doors. And what the fuck does he do? He opens the fuckin' window. We were nearly finished in there anyway. But when he set the dinger off, I jumped out the window, and when I was running across the garden, yer man and yer one were drivin' in. The cunt knocked me down . . . I got nicked about half an hour later. I might go "not guilty" on it, 'cause they've got fuck all on me. They didn't even get any money or jewellery back. The owners didn't get a good look at me, 'cause it was dark. I'm back up on it next week. This gear's all right on the foil, isn't it?'

'Yeah. How long is yer bird pregnant?'

'I don't know. About two months she reckons.'

'How long are ye out of Wheatfield?'

'About three and a half months . . . This gear's finished. Where will I put this foil?'

'Fuck it in the bin.'

I'm nicely stoned now. Then we hear the bell ringing and start getting our gear into the mouth in case it's the Old Bill.

Anto goes to the front door and asks who it is. I hear him opening the front door. I hear the door closing again, and then I hear the two voices coming in through the hall. I look up and see Anto and John in front of me. 'All right, John, what's happening?'

'The eyes on ye. It must be good smack.'

'No. I had a drop of phy. I'm celebrating.'

'What've you got to celebrate?'

'His bird's up the stick.'

'It's about time you stopped shooting blanks.' The two of them get a giggle out of that. John's about five-foot-four. Roughly the same as myself, although he has more weight on him. I'd say he's about seven stone and always looks clean and tidy.

'What're ye doing here, John? I wasn't to meet ye for an hour yet.'

'Same thing you are. Getting stoned . . . Give us four quarters, Anto.'

We make small talk between us while John gets two of his Qs into him. Anto is stoned and on a cleaning buzz.

'Right, lads. I'm off. John, will ye come down to me Ma's at ten o'clock?'

'Yeah, tell Claire I said hello.'

'Yeah, see ye later . . . See ye tomorrow, Anto.'

'Don't forget me money.'

'Yeah, yeah, yeah!'

I put the gear in me mouth as I'm going out the door. I've only walked a few feet from the flat when a dick car pulls in front of me. Two coppers jump out. Smelly Breath and another copper. He was about five-foot-ten. Fat. He had a tractor tyre, never mind a spare tyre. 'Right, Robert. Empty the pockets.'

'You want them emptied, you fuckin' do it.'

'I heard you got knocked down last week.'

'So did I, but I didn't remember it happening.'

'I'd say it was you all right. You were robbing the place blind. Now empty your pockets!'

I tell him to empty them as I put me hands on the car and spread me legs. They hate when you do that.

'Have you any needles on you?'

'Yeah.'

'What pocket are they in?'

'Put yer fuckin' hand in and find out.'

'Go on, get outta here, you little bollox.'

'Ah, do ye not want all the drugs I have in me pockets?'

'I'm going to catch you coming out of a window one of these days and you won't know what hit you, you little scumbag.'

'Well, I hope you're a good climber, because I prefer roofs these days.'

'You just might fall off one sometime.'

'Yeah, and you might fall with me.'

He didn't like that one. He gets back into the car and drives off.

I get into my house and I'm very surprised to see that there is no one in. I think I'll roll a joint. I stick three skins together, put some tobacco in them and goof off. I must have been there like that for about half an hour. Then my bird, Claire, comes in and wakes me up. 'The fucking state of you. You wanna do something with yourself before your Ma comes back. She'll kill ye if she's sees you.'

I go to the sink and throw some water on me face to wake me up.

'What time are you meeting John at?'

'He's coming down about ten. But we won't be going off until about one or two.'

It's late afternoon. We're in the sitting room on the sofa. Telly's on. But I don't even know what's on.

'I'm going up to Mary's in an hour. I'll be back down about twelve, so I'll see ye before you go out. You should go up and lie down for a while. Your Ma'll be back from work soon.'

'Yeah, I think I will. Will ye roll this joint.' I hand her the skins. They're falling apart. The tobacco I put in them is all over the table.

As she sits down beside me, she says, 'Look, you're that stoned, you can't even roll a joint . . . Listen, love, I'm not trying to get in your head, but you have to stop taking this shit.' But I'm not really listening. I'm already on another goof. She snaps me back out of it with a slap on the back of the head. 'It's pointless me talking to you when you're in this state.'

'C'mere and gis a kiss, love,' I say while putting my arm around the back of her neck.

'I'm going to get you up early in the morning, and before ye put any drugs into you, we're going to have a talk. You have to get off that gear, Bob.'

'Easier said than done.'

'Didn't I do it. I haven't touched the shit in months.'

'Yeah, but you were only on it for a couple months.'

'Bobby, don't give me that shit. You're only out of prison a few months . . . Go on upstairs. Your Ma'll be back any minute and I want to get your mess cleaned up before she comes back. I'll come up to you before I go.'

I give her a big kiss and make a big effort to climb the stairs. I go into my bedroom and go over to the corner and put the hi-fi on. All of the walls are covered in posters. Mostly birds with very little on. I plonk myself on me bed and put a spark to me spliff. Mark Knopfler is pumping out the sounds of his guitar through the speakers. Next thing I know, I'm in another goof.

It's very hard to describe this feeling. People have asked me to describe it many times, but I just can't find any words. It's like acting in a film, reading the book of it and watching it all at once. That might sound strange and weird, but it's the best I can do.

Next thing I know is I'm being snapped out of it by someone

shouting my name. 'Bobby! Ah for fuck sake, I only bought ye that jumper last week!'

I look down and there is a hole the size of a tennis ball in the middle of my jumper. It's still smouldering and the smell of it is horrible. I jump up and tear it off me and scrunch it up to put it out.

ALI BABA

I would like to thank
Marsha Hunt, for all her time and dedication
          She's One in a Million
Without her we could have never had done it.

And also My mother and family who my
      mother struggled to bring us up since the
death of my farther in 1985.
                  THANKS MA.
                      (ALI BABA)

It was Saturday night. About 12.30. A nice humid night. The whole house was very quiet. Everyone in bed.

I was sitting in the parlour with the younger cousin Tony. He's my dad's brother's son and was reared by my granny. He's like my younger brother. He looks up to me. Always did. We can tell each other things and it doesn't go any further. He used to come everywhere with me when we were younger. Sometimes, I had no choice. He'd whinge, 'Can I come too?'

'No,' I'd say, and then before you'd know it, he'd smack ye with a brick and ye'd have to give into him.

We came into the parlour from watching telly in the kitchen.

I sleep in me parlour. I won't sleep in me bedroom where me two brothers sleep, because me older brother is a scruffy fucker. He has the bedroom in chaos. In bits.

The parlour is where I sleep. And Tony, if he's in the house. It's my little bedroom with me black and white telly. I got it for nothing. Only two stations.

Tony was on the sofa and I was sitting on the chair. Chillin' and goofin'. The television was just fuzzing. We didn't notice it was still on. The curtains were still open, and you could hear people coming home from the pub. Getting out of taxis. A few common mouths. The neighbours from hell.

So Tony and me were just sitting there talking. We weren't talking about the usual bullshite of where we were going to get money, because we had twenty-eight lids in the pocket. We were stoned and felt all right. Happy because we had the price of three packets.

'Well, Tony, at least we won't have to get up early in the morning looking for money.' Sunday is a cunt for money. Ask anybody. 'Tomorrow won't be too bad. We have twenty-eight pounds. I'm not complaining.'

'Neither am I.'

I get the blankets and quilts from behind the armchair in the corner. He asks me for the sofa and, as usual, I give in to him.

'And don't forget,' Tony says, 'if you're up early, give me a shout.'

The only light there is is on the moon and the two cigarettes that's smoked before we go to sleep.

I sleep with the windows open to listen out for the police, because I'm on the run. I'm expecting the police any day now, because I never turned up for my court appearance. They'd only surrounded the house two weeks before, looking for a cash box. I was in the neighbours when they were raiding me house.

Sunday morning, me mother came into the parlour to wake me up like she does every other morning to see if I want to get up early. She pushed me shoulder.

'What time is it, Ma?' I'm not dying sick. I'm a bit groggy. The sun is beaming in through the window. I could hear the telly on in the kitchen. Cartoons. So I knew me nephew Michael was in there.

'It's a quarter past nine. Should I wake Tony up?'

I look over at him snuggled up under the quilt in a deep sleep, and I say, 'Leave him.' And I got up and walked to the kitchen.

Michael was sitting on the two-seater. He's me eldest sister's child. The eldest grandchild. And he stays in me mother's house every weekend.

I can smell chicken in the oven, because me Ma gets up early every Sunday and puts the dinner on. Gets the meat ready.

She asked, 'Are ye not getting washed?'

'I'll get washed when I get back.' I don't tell her I'm going down to the flats. But she knows.

'Ye never used to be like that. Will ye not comb your hair?'

Me mother's English. She had seven kids and was a widow at thirty-seven. She'll be fifty at Christmas. She used to ask, 'Is it my fault you're strung out? Did I drive you to it?'

She gave me life. I gave her hell. Years ago, when I was young, I was a little mammy's boy. Even me Da used to say that. I think all blokes are, but they won't show it. I love me mother, but I never tell her.

I look in the mirror and put me hands in me hair and squeeze it down. I'm only thinking of one thing and that's heroin. When I get back I got all day to get washed and enjoy that dinner. Me Ma's a wonderful cook and the smell of chicken is stuck to me nostrils.

I was at the mirror in the hall at the bottom of the stairs. It's a wonder that mirror is still fuckin' standing. There's always fighting in the house, and there's many a time my sister wanted to break it.

'I'm going out. I won't be long.'

'Where are ye goin'?'

'Don't ask . . . I won't be long.' Then I said to meself, 'Just hope I get down the flats and back all right. It's full of police down there.'

I'm going down to Fatima to score heroin.

FIDDLER

Dawin Farrell : The only Constant is
change and this book has changed our lifes I hope
it changes your perception of ours.

to Marsha for being honesty. to my OCD RIP - and most of all
to my Mother who give me Life is still the life / breath.
Finally Fuck the Sheep and beware of Leaders.

I am sitting in my cell and it's 1.15 on a Friday afternoon. God help me get through another day. I have been here for six months now and have another three to go. This is the most testing time of my life. It's a test I cannot pass, so I try to limit the damage. There's no physical threat in here, if you play your cards right. But the thing is, you have to try not to go off your head.

How I ended up in here is that on Wednesday, the 4th of June, '98, exactly six months ago to the day, I woke up in my friend's gaff in Rathmines. I was sleeping there, because me Ma is gone to Butlin's with my sister and her kids. She won't let me stay at home on my own, because she knows I would probably sell the TV or anything else I need to sell to get my gear. Or I'd have the place full of people turning on, just so I could get a turn on off them.

I hate staying in other people's houses. I feel like a tramp. Like a lost soul with nowhere to go. It's been like this the past fourteen years; stayin' in hostels, other cunts' flats, me Own's house (if I can play me cards right with her) . . . stairs of flats. Anywhere. I don't give a bollox where I sleep, 'cause it's not a matter of sleep. It's just killin' time for the next turn on.

I fucking hate being like this, but at this stage, after fourteen years of using, it's a matter of being sick or going without drugs. So, I don't give a bollox, I just want gear. It's not a matter of life or death. It's more important.

Anyway, that 4th of June, six months ago, I woke up on the sofa in the front room of me mate's gaff having slept the sleep of a junkie. It's not sleep, 'cause you're always aware you have to wake to face another day.

There was a big picture of Buddha on the wall. I wonder what he thinks of me with track marks all over me body. Hard blood left from needles from tryin' to get a hit. Decrepit body. Guilty mind. Seedy thoughts. I want to cover the picture, so he can't see me life's a fuck up. Jesus, my soul feels like a ton in weight. And my body is weak. It's full of holes from trying to get a hit in me feet, hands, legs, neck. Nowhere is sacred.

I put on me runners that me mate gave me. The bleeding smell off them. And the socks are hard from dirt. To a junkie, water is like bleach. It takes the stone off you. It's like you're allergic to it. So I hadn't washed in weeks. Just me face and hands, if I'm bothered enough.

I never hang around in gaffs too long, unless I have gear on me, but I hadn't, so I had to go score. I always felt like a thief fucking off from these houses before anybody was awake, because I couldn't have no distractions or delays.

I had ten valium 5 milligrams which should calm me down and hold me till I score. I am lucky. I have a score on me, so I can get a straightner without going out stroking.

I hate having to go off robbing when I'm dying sick. It's a model for a kamikaze. I didn't give a bollox when I was sick – I'd do anything for money. Take any chance. I'd go straight into a shop, put a few pairs of Levis up me shirt. Alarms on them? – Fuck it. I'd be like a pregnant woman leaving and wait until there was no security at the door, or they weren't looking out, or talking or something. Then I'd make my move. BANG! The alarms would go and I'd fucking tear along the street to get a good head start.

Most of the time no one comes after you, 'cause I think they're so surprised, they don't know what's going on, or else they don't give a bollox. If they do chase you, they'll get a syringe pulled out on them, and they're afraid of their lives of that.

So on the 4th, I didn't have to go out and do a kamikaze, 'cause I had a few bob on me, and I could have gone down to Heuston Station as well to get twenty mils of blue phy on the Eastern Health Board bus. But it's not worth a bollox and too much hassle. It wouldn't even stop my sickness. And I have enough for two quarters anyway. With the valium and the gear, I should get a nice straightner out of them, even a goof.

I head down Meath Street to score and hope there's someone with gear this early, 'cause I hate going to Fatima to score. Fatima is where most of the gear in Dublin is sold. It's red hot and there's loads of cunts doing rips up there, especially first thing in the morning. You could end up buying gear and getting rat poison instead. So I stick to Meath Street, 'cause I'm from there and know everyone around there.

I get to Meath Street and I see Martin Domorcain at the corner looking well suspect. 'What's the story, Martin? Anything around?' I say to him. The usual line used by anyone looking for drugs.

'No, I didn't see anyone. Do you want a few valium?'

'How much?'

'There's five valium, so fifty pence each.' I'll get eight and try to get the two quarters for sixteen pound. I'd rather have eight valium with my gear and take a chance on the two quarters for sixteen pound.

I chew the valium to make sure I get all of them into me. They'll calm me down till I score and I go looking for someone with gear now. It's raining out on the Coombe, and the breeze is cutting coming off Meath Street. It's bleak.

Most of the blokes and birds around here are strung out. There's a gang of them walking around looking for drugs or money for drugs. Young kids. Young fuckin' blokes. Women. Men. Everyone looking to score. You can spot them a mile away. They all have the same look as me imprinted in their eyes. Dejection. White faces. Bitter-looking. Skinny. Like Jews in a concentration camp I used to see on old *World at War* documentaries.

I don't remember how gear got such a hold around here or how it took hold so fast. It's like waking up one day and all of a sudden everyone is strung out. The worst of all is when you see a bloke you used to play Cowboys and Indians in your street with, and the two of you are strung out to bits, running around taking valium and smack and waiting to score.

I see a few people hovering around up the street and I know there's gear for sale up here. It's like a sixth sense I have. There's about fifteen people going into a side street with the bloke selling gear. He would sell it to them on the main street, no problem, but it's handier on a side street. They're all around him like vultures.

'Give us three' . . . 'Give us five' . . . 'Give us two quarters for this gold chain,' is all I can hear.

I know by the amount of bags people are scoring, he's going to be sold out any minute. There's a young girl in front of me about seventeen. I push her out of the way. She's not quick enough. Just standing there waiting. She mustn't be on the gear long or she'd be at the front herself.

I push me way up to him. 'Here,' I say, 'gimme two for sixteen pound, Paul.' As if I know him. And I'm saying to everyone else that his gear is lovely. This is a trick I use to make the guy think I know him.

I get them off him, no sweat. I know every trick in the book at this stage. Fourteen years of practice, I'd want to.

Lovely. I have my gear. Straight into the mouth. No one's getting this. Just another five minutes and I'll have it inside me.

Right, where will I go for a turn on? Sheener's gaff, I think.

I fly around the corner to his house, but there's no one in. Bollox. Right, I'll go down to Francis Street Church to the scout hall on the grounds of the church. It's been derelict the past four years, and it's being used as a shooting gallery.

I run. Jesus, I'm dying screaming for this turn on.

I have to get water, so I go over to the holy water and put my syringe in. I need this water for cooking up me gear.

The scout hall is falling apart. There's no door on it. The bang of shit in it is off the wall. Loads of used works lying around and burned tops of Coke cans used to cook up gear. It's fucking dark. So I light the candles that are there.

Right, a concrete block to sit on. Make sure there's no shit on it. Get my works out. My spoon. Lighter. Citric.

It's fucking freezing. I hope I can get a vein up. I put the gear on the spoon, holding it steady, my life depends on it.

Citric and water and heat it up. The gear dissolves. It's fairly dark. Looks like nice gear. Bollox. No filter for sucking up the gear. I don't give a fuck at this stage, I just want a hit. So I pick an old one off the ground and use that.

I try to get a hit in my hand. I have to stick the needle in about ten times and probe around for a vein. I'm panicking.

Then I see the crimson-red blood mixing with the brown water. My fear leaves me. I ram the gear in and feel a sting from the citric acid.

And then yes. I'm safe, till my next turn on.

CRIMINAL LIFE

EDGE

I want to thank Marsha
for Macking this Passoble
for me and everyone that
was involved

123

I Dedicate this to My Wife
Pamela and Kids
Alan Edgar

'You'd want to stop hitting me! I don't know nothing. I don't know what you're on about. I'd nothing to do with that robbery.'

'Yes you had. There's a witness.'

'Well get your fucking witness and stop hitting me. I've told you I've nothing to say to you people. Now I want to see my brief.'

All day and all that night I was questioned about a post office robbery I knew nothing about. I was really getting tired at this point when suddenly the door of the cell opened again and in walked four of the biggest bastards I've ever seen. 'Are you going to give this statement?'

'Fuck you. I'm saying nothing. I haven't done anything.'

'Let's give it to the bastard,' I heard one of them say.

I thought, 'Oh, no. Here we go again. Another fucking beating.'

I was sitting on the concrete floor. They started booting me up and down the cell like a football. I curled up like a ball and they went on hitting me for about five minutes. But it felt like forever. Kicking and punching me, using their little bleeding trick with the big books: one holds you down while the others beat you all over the body with the baton, using the big book so that they don't leave any marks on me.

It was one of the most frightening nights I've ever spent in a police station. I started thinking, is it worth it? . . . It has to be. I'm innocent. I did nothing wrong.

After they stopped beating me, I was lying on the concrete slab on the ground, looking up. My back was broke. Well, that's what I thought with the pain I was going through. I couldn't feel my legs or my arms. I just wanted to die. I lay there in the corner of the cell thinking, 'Will this ever end, because I can't take much more of it.' But I had to. I wasn't going to prison for something I didn't do.

All that night I was in pain, hoping they would give up. But no, after three hours, they came in again. This time with the sweet-talking method. They take out the cigarettes and offer you one and a cuppa tea. I refused everything.

'Fintan, if you sign this statement, you'll be out of here in three minutes. I will guarantee you that. All right? We know you did it. You know you did it. So what do you say? Have we a deal? Sign the fucking statement and you're out of here.'

I'm thinking, 'If I sign that statement, I'm going to prison for someone else's stupidity.'

'I told you before and I'll tell youse again, I have nothing to say to you people. I'm not pleading guilty to something I didn't do. Now can I see my solicitor? You're denying me my rights.'

'You have no fucking rights,' one of them said.

I knew I had. But there was nothing I could do about it, not until I seen my brief. Then they left me alone in the cell again. This time I wasn't hit by them, but still the minutes were like hours. The hours were like days. I couldn't do anything. I was like a spider caught in a web.

I couldn't sleep because of the pain I was in. But even so, I was afraid to go to sleep thinking they might come back in and thinking, what the fuck will they do next? Will they beat me or will they just talk to me again?

Hours passed.

With my legs in pain, I crawled over to the cell door and started kicking it till someone came.

About twenty minutes later, a copper said, 'What do you want?'

'I want to see the sergeant of the station. I need a doctor. Will you get the sergeant? I think me arm's broken.'

After about another twenty minutes, the door opened. In walked the sergeant. 'What's wrong, Fintan?' He knows me years. He was big with a big belly on him. The sort of sergeant that wasn't into cruelty. He was only coming on duty and didn't know what was goin' on himself, he said. I'm still sitting on the concrete floor. The light was on.

'I think my arm is broke. I want to see a doctor and I want to see my brief. I've been asking for him all night, but your so-called officers won't ring him for me.'

'When were you arrested?'

'Last night. Eight o'clock. What time is it now?'

'Six o'clock in the morning, and I've just come on duty myself.'

I didn't want to say I was beaten up, because he would have told me to go fuck myself. 'Well I've been questioned about something I know nothing about, and I want to know now if I'm going to be charged or let go?' At that stage there was only twenty-four hours they could hold you.

'I'll be back in a few minutes, Fintan, and I'll let you know.'

Suddenly, I was on my own again. Cold, lonely and frightened. What was going through me mind was were they going to start beating me again? I lay on the concrete bed and tried to go to sleep. But I couldn't sleep. By the sun coming through the little window above me, I guessed about two hours had passed. When I couldn't go to sleep, I started reading the graffiti. Looking for names I knew. I never write on the wall meself, because it's a true sayin' that you always come back to see it.

'Fintan,' the sergeant's voice said when the door opened again.

'What?'

'You can go now. I've been talking to one of the guards that arrested you and he told me on the phone there is no charge being brought against you.'

'What do you mean on the phone?' I was expecting them to still be in the police station.

'The guards that brought you in are gone home since six o'clock.'

'Well, fuck me,' I said to myself, 'After all that.'

I walked out of the cell. Well, just about. My legs, arms and back were still in pain. When me and the sergeant got to the jailer's cell, the sergeant said, 'Have you any property? Were there any rings, watches or jewellery taken off you?'

'No.'

'All right. Just sign that.' It was a form.

'What is it?' I said.

'Ah, just to say you weren't touched.'

That's a fucking good one.

'Sir,' I said, 'I don't mean to be smart, but I'm not signing anything.' Fuck me, I thought, it was all going to start again.

'Suit yourself. Let him out, officer.'

I was happy to be getting out. I'd been in twenty-four hours and was absolutely worn out. It was ten past eight in the morning and was sunny and warm. My house is fifty yards from the station. I made it home and told my wife what had happened to me.

TERRY

"Guilty Until Proven innocent"

Terry!

I dedicate this book,
to my fellow prisoners.
There's light at the end
of the tunnel.!.

Terry!

It all began on a horrible winter's night. We were out in search for money, so we could look after our deadly drug habit. It was about 11.30 p.m., very cold, windy and rainy. Every robber's dream. Us robbers love that kind of weather when we are working. It really helps a lot.

There was three of us. We met at a shooting gallery, in a flats complex in my area. It's a place we use for banging up or whatever. This particular flat was very well known, because three people ODd in it. My auntie was the first a few years ago.

The owner of the place, Shake, was in bits. The locals and the media labelled him 'Dr Death'. He'd had a motorcycle accident some time ago and it left him fucked up. Doctors had him on at least a hundred different tablets a day. But he used to take about two hundred and he would be so stoned on them, he'd be wobbling, had no balance and was always falling. Shake was a nice bloke. He'd say, 'Come on in. Happy turn on.' I don't know how he could think straight, let alone hold a conversation. Although he was very intelligent, everyone took advantage of him. When some junkie goofed off with a lighted cigarette, Shake ended up dying because of the fire. He jumped off the balcony, landed on his head, and never came round.

But ages before that happened, that's where the three of us met to make plans for breaking into a very large factory.

I can see the three of us on the roof taking the slates off to get into the attic. We entered the back of the building, collected tools I'd hidden the night before and climbed onto the lower roof of the back extension.

Passing up the tools, crowbars, chisels, screwdrivers, angle grinder, then we climb up the drainpipe to the main roof. When we got there, I pulled the tools in a coal sack up by the rope. I then started at the slates. Within minutes we were in the attic. I kicked in the plaster and dropped into the office. The two lads followed me and we gave the office a good search but found nothing we were interested in. So off to work we went, starting with the big safe.

We just cut the hinges off in five minutes, then wedged it open with crowbars. We got a small amount of money out of it but read the lodgement books and had a rough idea what was in the other safe and tried everything to get it open.

The lads kept saying, 'Come on! Come on, leave it! We'll never get that.'

But I kept working at it. I said, 'Look, if youse want to go, go now, 'cause I'm fucking stayin' until I get this.'

The two of them said, 'We'll wait on the roof. The office is too stuffy.' All the dust from the plaster ceiling coming in and then the fumes from the petrol grinder, you could just about breathe.

I couldn't get at the back of the safe, as they had it bolted to the floor. I've never seen anything like it – a big solid steel pipe coming up through the floor into the safe. It wasn't going to budge, so I tried cutting through it . . . If I'd had maybe another twenty blades for the grinder, then I might have got it . . .

I left it there and was so pissed off. All that poxy work for a couple hundred pound. I felt like burning the place down – if I can't have it, well no one's having it. I felt like a loser. What killed me was knowing what was in it.

The lads were screaming for a fix. So we went off, scored our gear and went to a house and had our fix.

Just when we had our fix, I asked the lads were they ready for our next job. The impression I got off them is that they were just happy with what we got. I explained the details about the next job but didn't tell where this place was. Just in case things went wrong and in case I got nicked. The lads said I'd never pull it off, and they bottled it. So this made me more determined. They called it a night. But I said to meself, 'Bollox this, I'm going to work me ass off tonight and relax for the week.' I told the lads I wasn't going to do it, but I had other ideas.

I went to my gaff and everyone was in bed except my dad. He was in the sitting room watching the TV and drinking a glass of Guinness and smoking his pot. I sat down with him for a few minutes and had a few Js with him.

So I went up to my bedroom, sat on a chair and turned on the lamp on my locker, pulled open the drawer and took out my drug kit. My girlfriend woke up as I was cooking up the brown. She asked if everything went okay.

'Everything's cool,' I told her.

After we got our gear into us, I told her I was going to the shop, that I wouldn't be long and off I went on the mission.

The target was a jeweller's in the middle of town facing the old police station.

So I picked up my angle grinder, hit the back lanes to this place. I got there about 4 or 5 a.m. The weather was just lovely; freezing and lashing rain and very windy. Nobody's hanging around.

Just opposite this shop was the old police station which was at the time under construction. So I went over to the site, got a workman's helmet and put it on my head. I also took the fencing the workman put around themselves. While working, I put this fencing around the jeweller's.

So, there I was in the middle of the main street with a workman's helmet on me head and working away at my job.

I cut through the shutters and then tapped the window in and helped myself to the trays of 'Tom', put it all in a sack and just got off side to somewhere safe.

For about four to five days, I was stuck with the 'Tom'. Someone grassed me up with the people I usually do business with, and I wasn't happy with the price other people were offering.

Three days after the stroke, I still had the 'Tom'. Me Mam was waking me up. Shaking my shoulder saying, 'The police are at the front and back door.'

'Let them in,' I told her and looked out my bedroom window and saw them in white boiler suits, metal detectors and shovels. My Mam left the room, and I opened my locker drawer and took out my emergency fix. It was in the gizmo (syringe), cooked and all.

I was taking the gizmo out of my arm when a few garda entered my bedroom. I got dressed, washed and then they handcuffed me.

They wrecked the house. Found nothing as usual. My dad thanked them for digging up the back garden. They dug the weeds up, me and dad were going to do it in the week. (Fair play to them, they were good gardeners. How do you think they got the name Garda?)

They then arrested me and charged me and got me remanded in custody. So I went to the High Court and got bail put on me. I sold some of the 'Tom' to pay it.

I haven't a clue why they charged me, as I knew they had fuck all on me. When I went for trial, it was fucked out of court. Like other cases they tried me for. What a memory looking at that Pig. Nearly crying when it was fucked out of court.

BRIE

For my Mam and everybody who's
helped me along the way, my
heartfelt thanks.

Brie

I can't remember the date.

I walked into the crowded portakabin, eyes averted to the floor, digging my nails into my palms, concentrating on the physical pain, hoping that would take away the mental anguish.

There was only two chairs in the small boxroom used for visits by social workers, the psychologist, and probation officers. The Commissioner for Oaths was sitting in one, so I took the other. He was an old, old man. Silvery grey hair, horn-rimmed glasses, wrinkled face, yet kind-looking. He had on an ill-fitting suit which made me feel sorry for him. His liver-spotted hands, skin thin as paper, all veins, started sorting out the papers. I didn't want to look up. I could feel the sympathetic glances from the officer and social workers. My ears burned, my heart was pounding so loud, I thought everyone would be able to hear it. Worst of all, I needed a cigarette. Not for the nicotine, but for something to do with my sweating hands.

I looked around and spotted an empty crisp packet, and a Jaffa Cake box but no ashtray.

'Do you mind if I smoke?' My voice was barely a whisper. Funny, I was thinking, 'What will they think of me if I start smoking? . . . Unfit mother and that sort of thing.' I lit up. Feeling a little more in control. The grey smoke drifted towards the Commissioner. I could hear him stifle a slight cough. 'Typical of a non-smoker,' I thought to myself. But fuck it, he'd just have to live with it. This felt like my funeral. The small prison welfare box soon filled with a blue haze.

Whilst he was reading the forms out to me, I kept glancing around the room. Under the table was an empty Jelly Tot packet. A toy train was discarded in the corner of the room. A teddy bear sneered at me from underneath a chair. I felt like asking it, 'What the fuck are you looking at?' But then they'd class me as mad altogether.

Jesus Christ! A gold pen in the Commissioner's arthritic-looking hand. A special pen for a special occasion. Doing things in style or what?

I could feel a trickle of sweat run down my side. With every question I felt nearer to tears. You're not going to cry, I told myself sternly. I bit my lip and could feel my eyes well with tears. 'One falls and you're done for, Brie,' I thought. I brushed it real quick with one finger and blinked quickly to spread the tears around, concentrated on the Jelly Tot packet, and lit up again.

Do they think I don't care, 'cause I'm not crying?

I'd have lung cancer before I got out of this poxy little box.

The Commissioner handed me his gold pen. My hand shook taking it. 'Just sign at all the Xs,' he said with a sympathetic smile.

I'm sitting there and loads of thoughts were racing through my head. But it's now – or never . . .

I could hear the social worker, a small, slightly built woman, clearing her throat as if to say, 'Don't back out now.' I was doing such a personal thing and it was so official. How could any of them have a clue about how I felt about what I was doing?

The social worker had no kids.

I took a deep breath and started writing my signature. My heart heavy with guilt. My face red with the shame.

'Unfit mother.' That's all I could think of.

But then I pictured her face. Her blond hair and blue eyes, her cheeky grin. My little girl.

Not for much longer. The final adoption papers. I signed all my parental rights away.

I know she's with a good family. They give her the love and care she needs. But that doesn't take the pain away. It just dulls it.

PAUL

I would LIKE TO THANK EVERY
body who was involved and
who put a lot of work and their
time into getting this book to
where it is now especially to
MARSHA HUNT who put great
effort and work into getting this
books established. THANKS A LOT
MARSHA WE WILL ALL MISS YOU AND
YOUR CLASSES UP HERE.

DEDICATED TO MY MOTHER PAULINE
FATHER, BROTHERS PATRICK, BARRY
& MARK and SISTER DENISE and
to nephew & niece SCOTT + NICOLE
also to SOMEONE who is SPECIAL
and a great Friend to me JANICE !

Paul Doyle

There is one thing that really triggers me off and gets my blood to boil, and that's every time I open the papers, and it always has something in them about child molesters and sex cases. And all that's been done and said about them is they are sick people and they need a lot of treatment for what they did to other people's lives. Whereas the likes of us ODCs (ordinary decent criminals) get a write-up in the papers after getting years for robberies and there is no treatment recommended for us for our drug problem which caused us to do the robberies. All we are classed as in public is scum, and that's not true. Whereas all them scumbags out there raping people and molesting innocent kids are just classed as sick and get more lenient sentences for their crimes than the ones we do for robberies and other minor offences.

PRISON LIFE

THE QUIET MAN

The more I see of the representatives of the people the more I admire my dogs.

The Quiet Man

I'd like to dedicate this story to my
family who have stuck by me through
this sentence.

The two of us were doubled up last February for a couple of weeks. He wasn't much to look at the first time I met him. About five-foot-eight, light build, brown hair. He hadn't a pick on him and couldn't stop yapping. That was my first impression of J.D. Doyle. I remember the first night . . . We were sitting there in the cell with no sounds. The bloke that had been in with me had taken the radio with him. Well, it was his, so what could I say?

'So what's your story, J.D.?' I asked. 'Where ye from?'

'Ballymun. Do you know the flats out there?'

'No. Never been.'

'Where are you from yourself?'

'Me, I'm from the country.'

'So you're a mulla. Is it true what they say about the people from the country? Ye know about the sheep an' all?'

'It's true about most of it but not all. So how long are you doing, J.D.?'

'Sixteen months for robbing a poxy push-bike. You'd rob anything when you're strung out, d'you know that?' He said he'd been strung out for the past twelve months.

I had enough for a couple joints that night. It broke the ice a bit. We stayed up till half one the next morning playing cards and talking. Time was going fast enough. We could hear the sound of the cleaners on the 1s doing the landing and MTV blasting from the telly at the end of D1.

'I'll see you in the morning, J.D. I'm banging on that light and getting me head down.' (Yeah, that little red light in the corner of the cell you have to stick on no matter what it is you want, whether it's to get out to the jacks or to turn off the lights to go to sleep. You'd think that they'd have a light switch in the cell, instead of having some cunt coming round when he feels like it to turn off the light for you. It's fucking ridiculous.)

J.D. didn't really want to go to bed. 'I'm dying sick, so I doubt if I'll get fuck all sleep,' he said. Now at this stage, I had heard lads on the landing talking about being dying sick, but I had never seen anyone coming off heroin myself. Not until J.D. I found it hard to understand what he was going through. I had no idea how bad he was feeling and didn't know what to say. All I could do was pity him.

I woke up the next morning at about eight o'clock and there was J.D. pacing up and down the cell.

'What are you doing up at this hour of the morning?' I asked him.

'I couldn't sleep. I'm not feeling the Mae West. I've been up for a couple of hours. I'm too sick to sleep.'

'It's just as well I had that bit of blow last night, or you'd have had me up with you.'

I got a radio in the shop that day. It was a small little white transistor. Not great but it done the job, so we had some sounds at least. It didn't really matter, 'cause J.D. was full of chat. He couldn't sit still for two minutes. One minute he would be at the end of my bed talking, then he'd be up on the bunk or opening or closing the window.

'What are you closing that window for, it's roasting in here.' The heat in the cells at that time was something else. I don't think the window had been closed all winter, because it was that warm with two in a cell.

'I'm freezing up here,' J.D. said. 'That's some breeze blowing through that window.'

'A minute ago you were telling me that the sweat was pumping out of you.'

'You don't understand what it's like comin' off gear. It does me warm one minute and the next I'd have a cold chill down me back. The aches are constant. Never stopping. I can't get any rest. You should count yourself lucky that you never had to go through withdrawals, because they're a pure bastard.'

'Yeah. I'm glad, because if I was going through what you are right now, I think I'd go off me head. It's bad enough you keeping me awake without me being dying sick too.'

Now I didn't mind any of this during the day. But at night it was another story.

'Here, take up that radio. The eleven o'clock news will be on in a minute. I'm going to get a kip. Don't have it too loud.'

'Nice one . . . Is that all right? It's not too loud is it?' he asked.

'No. It's cool.' I'm lying in bed with my head under the pillow and all I can hear is the squeak of the bunk over my head. 'Lucky it's not me up there,' I'm thinking, 'and if he doesn't stop moving about up there, I'll be lucky if I get to sleep tonight at all.'

Twelve o'clock news . . . One o'clock news . . .

'Ah for fuck sake. Not again!' Right across from me is J.D. curled

up into a ball on the lino floor. 'What time is it and what the fuck
are you doing with the mattress on the floor?' The cell isn't that big
when there're two mattresses side by side, and there's fuck all room
by the door. It would've been a bit awkward trying to step over him
if I'd have had to get up to have a piss during the night.

'I couldn't sleep on the bunk. It's too uncomfortable.'

'And did you get any sleep down there?'

'A bit. But not too much.'

It's not quite light outside but won't be long before a new day is
upon us. It was much brighter looking up from below with the
mattress gone from the top bunk. 'What time is it anyway?' I ask.

'About quarter to six.'

'Ah, Jesus, J.D., you're going to have to do something about
having me awake at this ungodly hour of the morning, and you're
keeping me awake half the night too.'

'Listen. I'm sorry. It's just that I'm not able to get any rest myself,
and I keep moving about to get comfortable.'

The guy had me head done in with all his moving around and
talking. Even when I was trying to read the paper, he kept inter-
rupting me as if I wasn't doing anything at all.

I usually go to bed about eleven every night, but now that J.D.
was with me, I was lucky to be asleep at one-thirty. 'J.D., will ya
turn down that radio a bit. I can't get to sleep with it.'

'Ah, sorry. I thought you were asleep already.'

'No fear of that,' I said to myself and I got to sleep only to be
woken up at about half six.

'Jesus Christ, not again. Turn down that radio, will ye!'

'Did I wake you with it?'

'No. I wake at this time every day. Just turn down the radio a
bit.'

I thought J.D. was all right, but I wasn't too sure if I could last
with not getting all my sleep. I didn't say anything to him, because
I could see he wasn't well.

'I might be getting a visit today,' he said, 'and hopefully, the bird
will bring us up a Q or two. I'll throw it in the tinfoil and ease the
pain for an hour or two.'

He got his visit that afternoon and got a bit of gear on it.

Back in the cell, he got out the tinfoil, sat down on the end of
my bed and proceeded to smoke the gear. As sick as he was, he

offered me a smoke, but I said, 'No, you're all right. You need it more than I do.'

After he'd smoked it, I asked, 'Now that you've got that in you, how do you feel?'

'I feel like "more"!' The two of us started laughing. J.D. said, 'That's the thing about gear. You just keep smoking and smoking, until BOOM, you're strung out. After that it's a constant runaround trying to score some gear or else robbing to get the money for it. That's all it is. Gear. Just gear.'

'Yeah, well, thank fuck gear isn't a problem where I'm from or the two of us could be dying sick here together.'

'Take some advice from me. Don't get into it. It's bad news.'

'How'd you get into taking gear in the first place?' I asked.

'It's not very hard to get into it when you're living in Dublin, because it's everywhere. And out there in Ballymun where I'm living, I'd say half the teenagers out there are on it. There's nothing else for them to do. Kids as young as thirteen and fourteen doing gear. D'you ever do it yourself?'

'Yeah. I did it a couple years ago when I was in England, but I never got strung out or anything.'

'Did you like it?'

'Yeah. It was all right.'

'I bet you thought it was more than all right. I bet you thought it was lovely.'

'Listen, I seen what it was doing to the people that I was around at the time, so I knew it couldn't be good. I remember me cousin picking me up from his mother's house where I was staying and driving me around the city and telling me about the way he was selling smack. He brought me back to the gaff that he was using to sell the gear from and said to the bloke who was selling to look after me, whatever I wanted.

'The first night I thought was it was all right. It was new to me so I was up for anything. But as the weeks wore on, I got to know some of the people coming in and out of the house pretty well and they were filling me in on what they had to do to get a few quid. I done that for six weeks and then got back on a plane to Dublin. I decided then I wouldn't get involved with gear.'

J.D. was in with me for two weeks and as the second week wore on, his sleeping pattern improved a bit. He didn't have me up so early, but he was still a bit reluctant to get his head down any way early, because he'd rather waffle the ears off me instead.

After J.D. left, I got another bloke in with me and luckily enough, he wasn't going through withdrawals.

I saw J.D. a few weeks later. He must have put on a stone and a half and I commented on how fat he had gone. He said, 'That's being off the gear for you.'

FRANCIS

inside a small boy smiled and I knew "francis"
had finally come home!

Thanks to Deirdre, Sara, my father, my mother, Roly Condra, Claire Jones and a lot of others for loving me when it was tough to.

Francis Condra.

It's lunchtime so the place is quiet. The silence is broken only by the sound of my radio. The ads tell of the approach of Christmas, all bells and Ho! Ho! Ho! I'm sitting here relaxing after lunch, which consisted of boiled potato and minced beef stew, smoking a cigarette and drinking a cup of coffee almost ritually.

The cell is thirteen by eight and is furnished with a steel bed and desk unit which is bolted to the wall; a toilet and sink are attached to the cut-off corner of the cell beside the grey door. The built-in mirror watches me, silently, made more suspect by the graffiti above it – 'two-way mirror – CAMRA'. The rest of the graffiti on the wall confirms that the previous occupants were drug addicts and in some cases semi-illiterate. The names are all in groups of nine:

Woody
Yogi
Robbie
Jay
Fonzie
Kavo
Whelo
Eric
Tupac

Nine at a time pass through this place, nine cells, nine addicts. You see, this is the drug rehab wing of the medical unit in Mountjoy Prison. Nine at a time on the six-week rehab programme seek to escape the Joy and drugs.

Photos. Sara, Deirdre, together, daughter and wife. They smile at me, the only reminders of the outside world. They remind me that there are people out there who care about this jailbird ex-junkie. They also bring back memories of the past and my failures as a father and husband.

'Don't quit' the plaque says. And I won't. Deirdre left it in for me. She also gave me the Native American dream catcher that hangs over the bed and the poster depicting the ten 'Indian' commandments that hangs on the wall.

The desk is divided into two sections by the towels that cover it. One, beige, is the food side; tea bags, sugar, milk, jam, crackers. I use this side as my kitchen-cum-diner. The other half is covered by a purple towel and is my office desk. Tapes, photos, plaque, pentagram, celtic cross, pens and writing materials. A pack of shag tobacco, skins and a zippo lighter lie on the border between both as if unsure which side they belong to.

The window is a narrow slit about two by five with regulation bars on the outside, no curtains. This is jail, after all.

I've been here since Saturday. Five days. Myself and eight others. We're beginning to gel as a group. There's Fran, Steven, Gerry, Jimmy, Brian, Sticky, John, Derek and me. We do group therapy every day. The prison authorities bring in facilitators from Coolmine, the most famous drug rehab in Ireland, Ana Liffey Project which is a drug rehab drop-in centre, and Ballymun Youth Project. So far, we 'know it all', and maybe that falsehood will be exposed over the next six weeks. Maybe us 'know-it-all-jailbird-junkies' will find we know fuck all, that's why we're here.

The guy from Coolmine talks about altering attitudes and perceptions. I know what he means. But the cell is thirteen by eight with a steel door and bars on the window. I think he means that we should see the real prison, the one inside ourselves, that we are internally imprisoned. Minds locked in by fucked-up emotions. Obsessions and compulsions acting as prison officers.

The drugs don't work as an escape route from that prison, they wear off and you wake up back in your self-made cell or maybe it's a self-made hell.

Anyway, it's Thursday lunchtime and we get our visits this afternoon. I expect my Da will be up. He's sound, my Da, although I didn't always think so. But getting clean has changed our relationship. He stood by me in my hour of need, whereas Christ – his Father forsook him on the cross. No, *my* Da never forsook me . . .

It's fourteen months now since I began my recovery. That's a good word, 'recovery'. Brings to mind car wrecks, and I was a wreck. But that's changing. The bodywork has been straightened out and the engine is being fine-tuned. By the time this wreck leaves Mountjoy Motors, he'll be good as new. Almost.

So, Marsha, you're sitting there reading this and probably thinking, 'Yeah, Francis, but what's the point?'

Well, the point is this – it's lunchtime and I'm bored in here, so I write to you, to give you an insight into this jail shit.

This is no big deal. It's security parking of human beings. It's a mundane, monotonous thing. Writing helps pass that time and being locked up alone in a cell eighteen hours a day concentrates the mind. You start to see things in a different way. Altered perceptions. So it's not just a guy sitting in a cell. It's much more. It's home. It's bedroom, sitting room, dining room and bathroom all in one. It's life concentrated and condensed like Carnation tinned milk.

I'm one of the lucky ones. I'm getting help. Most don't. They are parked, then let out to double park, get towed away and get security parked again.

Wrecks.

Me, I'm out in twenty months and I won't be back. It's not that this place is bad. It's not, and it actually grows on you. I won't be back because I have a life; a child, a wife, hopes, dreams. All that shit. But mostly the motivation to alter my perceptions. And as long as I hold on to that key, I can escape my own prison, so I'm not liable to do the shit that results in me being security parked again.

The prison service didn't reform me, my higher power done that. She would have done it without prison.

JOHN

I had the gear the night before. Me usual four for fifty in Ballymun. It was muck. Never could hold a Q for the next day, always threw the four onto the spoon. I woke up at six the next morning. The minute I opened my eyes that bastard 'monkey' was in me ear again lookin' for his fuckin' breakfast. 'Feed me, feed me, feed me.'

I knew I'd be in bits by the time I got me few quid and scored. I wanted a TO as quick as possible to shut the cunt up for a while.

I didn't even wash or shave, put my gizmo, citric and spoon in me pocket and got a bus into town. The shops would only be open when I got there after nine.

I was after makin' too much money already out of this place, so I took a chance, though I'd been caught twice already in the space of a few years. I ended up doin' a kamikaze, even though I knew they just got a new dome camera in for shoplifters. I knew I'd be caught again but just prayed it wasn't that day.

I always took about a hundred and eighty quids' worth of CDs at a time. They were easy to hide and easy to sell. I was lucky to have a buyer in town. A fifteen-minute walk from the southside of the Liffey to the northside, and I get fifty or sixty quid for them.

But I wasn't so lucky that day. The security men were watching, waiting for me to make a mistake.

After a ban garda charged me in Pearse Street station, she found a committal warrant and found out I was 'on me toes' from the Joy. I was bollocked. The desk sergeant put me works in the plastic box for used gizmos, me citric and spoon went into a brown envelope, they were bringing me to court at 2 p.m. They wouldn't get me a bleedin' doctor for a drop of 'magpie' and told me I'd be looked after in the Bridewell.

'The Bridewell, my bollocks!' I thought. Them dirtbirds wouldn't get you a doctor if you were half dead. They'd give you fuck all but abuse. I was starting to panic.

After listening to me without taking his eyes off his books, the fat pig behind the desk in the Bridewell looked at me like I was a piece of dirt and said, 'Doctor? You'll get no fuckin' doctor in here. Who do you think you are? Youse junkies are like a bunch of fuckin' sissies. Youse want a doctor for everything from boils on yer arses to pimples on yer mickeys.' He got a giggle from the other muppets that stood around in their uniforms.

I was in the height of it now, too sick to argue with the cunt.

When he saw me take me empty wallet out of me brown envelope with me spoon and citric still in it, he said, 'Search him for needles. The lining of his coat as well.'

I slipped me citric down me jocks before he came from behind the desk, 'cause it's like gold dust in the Joy.

I don't know how long I was in that big, poxy concrete cell in the Bridewell before they brought me through the underground tunnel to Court 46. I was getting sicker by the hour. The court was packed when I walked up the stairs from the dock. I had a feeling I'd be wasting my time asking the judge for a doctor, but it didn't stop me.

I told him I was sick from heroin and needed a doctor.

He made a useless fuckin' order that said I was to be treated in the Joy when I got there. He should have used it for wiping his arse, 'cause I knew from before that my chances of getting phy in the Joy that day were slim and none. The Joy have their own rules when it comes to phy.

In through the same grey steel gates I'd walked out of the year before. Here I go again . . .

I was praying there'd be someone I knew in the holding cell with gear. I was left sitting in the little room on the right. The payphone on the wall said, 'Officers use only'. I told the other two prisoners that were there to keep watch while I dropped 20p in. That left me with sixty-three pence to my name.

When I rang me Ma's number, me brother answered.

He had a bit of a habit himself, so he knew the score. He had no fuckin' money, so he wouldn't get up to me early.

I hung up.

I took me belt and wallet out of the envelope, then crushed it up with me spoon still in it and fucked it behind the door. I put me bag of citric where the monkey puts his nuts.

The sickness was coming in waves. Getting stronger, lasting longer. Why did I get strung out again?

The minute I got to reception, it was nearly time to fall in after tea. There was no way I was going to get any phy till the next day. They'd have to test me piss sample to make sure I was a junkie. I started screaming for the medic and told him about the judge's order. He laughed.

'It doesn't matter if you crawl through the gate on your hands and knees dying sick,' he said, 'you know the story. You have to wait twenty-four hours. Like everyone else.'

I walked away from him to the bench at the back of the room to lie down. I wished the floor would open and swallow me. Me monkey was chattering in me ear again. 'Even a prison ten-dollar bag will do, and you'll be brand spanking new.' He wouldn't shut the fuck up.

After reception I was back in prison clothes and brought to the dreaded holding cell in the base. The Joy was packed. I went in and sat on the wooden bench as the screw slammed the door behind me and locked it. There were already eight fucking bodies there, sitting around.

I didn't know anyone. I scanned their faces but none looked like junkies. There was a black bloke in for breaking a barring order. There was a fat farmer in for not paying a fine. Three Northern Ireland heads in for getting caught with hash at the Verve gig in Slane, and another fella sitting on his hands, looking at his shoes. Just me fuckin' luck.

After half an hour me head was fucking melted.

I waited and waited and got worse and worse.

Into the jacks for a piss, I saw a tinfoil cake tray with black burn marks underneath and blood squirted on the wall and ceiling, bits of ripped cigarette filters and empty gear bags. All signs of junkies that had been there before.

I think, 'Fuck this for an act, I'm not staying here all night to listen to all these fuckers snoring in their sleep.'

Every vein in me body was screaming for a turn on or a line or even a snort. Anything to stop the pain.

I started banging the cell door with me fists till a screw came and looked in the spy-hole. I told him to get me an ACO, assistant chief officer.

'What do ye want him for?'

'I'm signing meself into the pad. I'm coming off gear and I want out of here, right? So just get him, will ye!'

The ACO came with a big motherfuckin' screw on each side of him. They probably thought I was off me Johnny Walker. The pad is for punishment. Nobody asks to go in, but there was no benches and no bodies. A cell to myself for the night till I get my phy. I was dying sick and needed to be on my own. More than twenty hours since my last TO and I was in tatters. Me body was turning to shite. Me stomach was churning, me eyes watering and me nose running. I stated me case to the ACO.

He had a smirk on his face when he told them to take me to the pad.

When I got there I couldn't believe me ears. The screws told me to strip down to me jocks!

I said, 'Are yez fuckin' winding me up or what? I'm going through cold turkey as it is, and it's bleedin' freezing in there. Sure, I'm going in voluntarily, and I'm making a bit more room for yez in the holding cell.'

'It makes no odds,' they said. 'That's not what the pad is used for.'

'Then fuck that. I'm going back to the holding cell, if that's the case.'

'I'm afraid you can't,' they said, 'the ACO has you signed in, and you can't get out till the doctor or governor signs you back out in the morning. You're in the base of Mountjoy Jail, son, not renting a flat.'

'Fuckin' scumbags,' I thought. 'They can see by looking at me that I'm in bits. That's why they were picked to work down in the base. 'Cause they're cold-hearted cunts, the pair of them.'

It was bad enough going into the pad without having to strip in front of them as well. They made me feel lower than a poxy snake. They had no fuckin' shame at all as they stood there like fuckin' lords with their hands on their hips. It was no use arguing with these fuckers in the state I was in. They had never heard of compassion. They were there to do what they done best, intimidate.

PUMA

There no point in haveing your Wealth if you have not got your Health.

I Would Like to Dedicate this to my Family and most of all my two Daughters With all my Love. Puma

It was a dry night. It wasn't cold, cold. It was a nice evening, but you'd still put your coat on. I was out in the yard watching a game of football. And I can hear one prisoner sayin' to another, 'Did you see 'im?' And two blokes just come into the prison are sittin' on the bench and they're lookin' up and down fairly tense. They've got prison service clothes on them. It was roughly about six o'clock, because the game had started. I was asked to play, but I didn't 'cause I was waiting on a haircut. Messin' with the ball on the sideline, my head was bleedin' flyin'.

The yard is small, half the size of a football pitch. The surface is tarmacadam, and there're four spotlights coming down on it from the wing and surrounding it is a fifteen to eighteen-foot wall with spinners, coiled razor wire.

The players are roarin', shoutin', callin' for the ball. Banks and Tee are in front yellin', 'G'won, give us the fuckin' thing.' And off the yard, a few steps down in the basement, shoutin' and laughin' is coming out of the recreation room.

What was goin' on in my mind was that my cell-mate Joe was willing to split a small prison ten-pound bag with me, but there was really only enough for one. He's trustworthy. Always been somebody I could rely on in any situation. We've been very close since I was twelve, and he would have been about nine. We had our first JLO together and had been cell-mates over the years. But heroin fucks up relationships, because if you're into drugs, seven out of ten of your visits consist of drugs. One cell-mate gets a visit and the other gets left out. It was going to lead to trouble, because it was comin' to the point that meself and Joe would be sittin' in the cell and all the time talkin' about gear and who'd be gettin' a visit.

I was getting paranoid. Getting a buzz. Then getting freaked . . . I was after having sixteen months of getting drugs on visits. Waitin' on this day. Waitin' on that day. Phone calls. Planning.

You go out on your visit, you get your drugs, and you come back in and everybody on the landing is like flies on honey.

I was gettin' hash all the time and Joe'd say, 'What's the story with the hash for tonight? Is somebody gettin' a visit?' He knows I give it out to blokes who also get hash on their visits.

You take drugs in here, the time goes faster. The only thing I want to know about is more drugs. So I put me name down for the detox unit, because of the drug situation and the way visits go. If I'm gonna give up drugs, the best place to start is in jail. It's even harder to get off drugs on the outside. If I can give it up in here, I'll have a couple months clean and can survive it better. Everyone I know in my area is either strung out or selling drugs or up to something drug-related. I won't be socialising with them . . . I'll go to the pub and have a few pints and go home and won't be in that vicious circle . . .

The detox unit is in the medical unit. There's three landings, the 1s, 2s and 3s. Each landing is split in half, and in each half, you've got nine cells. There's a snooker table, television, video . . .

Off the gear I'm more mature, more responsible. I'm stronger-headed and stop and think before I react. I'm more of a loveable person. I'm more sympathetic. Whereas when I'm stoned, it goes in one ear and out the other. On the gear, I'm on me own buzz. Me own.

This is gonna be the last chance I get to give up gear altogether. The last chance in my eyes.

The detox unit consists of blokes that's been abusing drugs in the main jail. The programme is basically about you – where you're weaned off heroin with methadone and given a sleeping pill at night. It's about counselling, about sittin' down with the counsellor. They have people from the outside coming in that run rehabs on the outside. Like Coolmine. They're giving you the help that you need to get off the drugs.

The habit I have is only a prison habit. The gear we get on visits is shite. I've been over here in detox since Friday evening. Seven days. There's no pressure. I feel more relaxed. No shaking or hot and cold sweats, and I haven't even thought about a visit or thought about gear. Today is the last day of getting phy . . . I know deep down I don't want any more drugs. I just feel good.

I'm at it ten years. I'm twenty-five. I'm startin' to get old. Starting to realise I'm an adult. Not a young fella. And I'm after missing out on the years . . . I never really socialised in a pub until 1997 when I got out of prison and knocked gear on the head for three months. Plus, like, I've got two kids.

For the time they've been around, I can only remember spending two Christmases with them . . . I've been out, but I can only remember once putting a Fisher Price kitchen and wardrobe together with mirror and drawers . . . I can remember that

Christmas, but I can't even remember the first birthdays, that first candle and the pretty dress on.

Although I know I brought them to the park, I brought them to the pictures, I brought them to the zoo, I brought them to the horse and carriage, to the horse fair, I have no early memories of them. They never wanted for anything, always had money to go to the shop and have a little party with their friends in the bedroom. To McDonald's . . . I got them names on their bracelets. I got them the best of everything. Designer stuff. I wouldn't go near Dunnes Stores.

I bought them and gave them every possible thing I could but the love they should have got from a father. There should have been me clear-headed, givin' them love. But it wasn't. I would say it was false love, because ninety-nine per cent of the time I was stoned. To me now it wasn't like love a hundred per cent. There was something fake. It was the gear. It was the heroin. It was the drugs.

YOGI

Who's the wasters now
Mrs fitz. /HA fuckin HA
yog!,
Tommy.g.

This is dedicated
to all the prisoners
in Irish Prisons

yogi

My mind is racing. The demon is screaming. My body is aching. I'm in a junkie's nightmare. Cold turkey.

Gear, gear, gear runs through my mind.

I can't sit still. Have to do something. Walk, sit, jump. Into bed, out of bed. Oh ye bastard, go away.

Pacing a cell fifteen foot long, seven foot wide, I must have walked ten, fifteen miles by now, and I'm still no nearer to where I want to go – out – score some gear, cook it, filter it and inject it. Just to take the pain away.

My bowels are playing up. Over to the piss-pot again and I reckon I will squeeze one more piss into it.

The cell-mate is asleep by now. Oh, I wish I was him in a deep sleep. His snoring is wrecking my head. I want to smack him with the piss-pot. 'Shut up, ye cunt!'

More walking. More pacing. More thoughts.

The screw has just looked in on me. He must think I'm going off my head, walking up and down the cell at three o'clock in the morning. It's a long night and there's longer to go.

I jump back into bed. Lying down, thinking, thinking, thinking . . . I jump up. I must have slept for a couple of minutes, because I forgot my thoughts. Even if it was only for a couple of minutes, it was a relief.

I smack my arms off the wall again. I just want to break them to see if that will ease the pain I'm feeling.

It's starting to get bright out . . . I'm nearly there. Nearly through one night of it and I still have a few nights ahead of me. But I don't worry about them. I'm just worried about now. Today. Will I get a visit? Will I get some gear on it? Will the pain go away?

I can hear the master locks. It must be seven o'clock now. Another hour to go to a fresh prison day. But the only thing different in every prison day is your thoughts. It's like deja vu over and over again.

Eight o'clock. I can hear the screws coming along the landing doing their counting. I'm nearly there. But I think, 'I'm nearly where?' Nowhere, there, where.

I think I just want the door open.

I hope that today goes better than yesterday.

I'd Like to dedicate
this Poem, to a few of
my friends, That is not
with us today.

Terry !

People just don't understand the word addicted: it's another word for 'bolloxed'. Once you pop, you just can't stop. First thing in the morning, you're batting needles into your arm just to take away the sickness. Who wants this life? Ninety per cent of junkies are from the lower-class areas.

ODE TO THE JUNK YARD

A turnkey, a gizmo, some powder to mix,
A spoon and a filter, then cook your own fix,
Then tighten the turnkey, a vein will appear,
Now stick in the spike and let's ride out of here.

This new world you've entered, there's nothing that's real,
But your mind it is numb, and no pain can you feel,
Then you walk round all day with one thing on your mind,
'Where will I get money for that fix the next time?'

Then your body starts sweating, but you're feeling so cold,
You're addicted to drugs and your habit grows old,
What you thought you could handle is out of control,
And now to the Devil you would sell your own soul.

A ten bag, a twenty, a napp for your high,
By the needle you live, and by it you'll die,
You won't be remembered and what will they say?
That was only a junkie who ODd today.

Terry!

175

I Dont like writeing because it was and is froce on you as You attend school as a kid and the teacher get to say Whet's right and wrong and your not really into it but the say it good for you and your future but i think Puting Pen to paper can get you into trible.

Its time for a change.

Time for me now is like being in Limo I could probably write about anything but time Its time for a change The days are getting shorter.

Were in class that's in the Prison.

Puma